C000282822

DOLCE VITA

DOLCE VITA

A NOVEL

Iseult Teran

Flamingo

An Imprint of HarperCollinsPublishers

Flamingo
An Imprint of HarperCollins *Publishers*,
77–85 Fulham Palace Road,
Hammersmith, London W6 8JB

Published by Flamingo 1999
1 3 5 7 9 8 6 4 2

Grateful acknowledgement is made for permission to reprint excerpts
from the following copyrighted works: 'Loving Arms' © 1972 Almo
Music Corp., USA; Rondor Music (London) Ltd., SW6 4TW.
Reproduced by permission of IMP Ltd. 'Don't Fence Me In': words
by Cole Porter © 1944 Harms Inc., USA. Warner/Chappell Music
Ltd, London, W6 8BS. Reproduced by permission of IMP Ltd.
'Anything Goes': words and music by Cole Porter © 1934 Harms Inc.,
USA Warner/Chappell Music Ltd, London, W6 8BS. Reproduced by
permission of IMP Ltd.

ISBN 0 00 225708 4

Printed and bound in Great Britain by Clays Ltd, St Ives plc.
Typeset in Electra and Escript by
Palimpsest Book Production Limited, Polmont, Stirlingshire

For my husband Nick
and my son Felix

CHAPTER I

PARIS, SEPTEMBER 1989

Nearly two hours sitting in the studio with Henri, trying to keep the subject off sex. Henri is an octopus from Martinique. He has dreadlocks and five brothers. They live next door with their mother and two little girls – his. They don't have a bathroom. I'm in a huge studio, alone, with a hot and cold shower and a washing machine. Henri has women round in the day because in the evening his family all sleep in their one room in bunk beds. He's an insomniac. At night he likes to come round, talk to me and see if he can get inside my knickers. He is usually so stoned his stories trail into unbelievably dull monologues that go nowhere. Sometimes, just to shut him up, I think: should I kiss him? Intuitively I know that if I were to kiss Henri, I could kiss goodbye to my future. He has no twinkle, he can't be on my list.

I am saved from his hairy clasp by the doorbell. Running down the stairs, I notice that my dress is ripped. Through the spy hole in the door I see a pair of magnificent lips. I look at them for a while, then let them in, but only after jamming the mackintosh cupboard full of clothes, laundry, plates and something that nearly breaks my toe as I kick it.

When I opened the door I saw this person who hurt my insides to look at; I wanted to throw myself at him, so I jumped into the tattooed arms of the bass player who'd brought him. Once they were inside the studio, I sat The Lips where I could look at him with ease. I didn't want to listen to him.

'So . . . it is very 'ard for me being a prince . . .'

So he's a prince: blah blah blah. Italy's full of so-called princes too – if you really want to impress me, buy me a Burger King. Feed me. Here I am in Paris, determined to enjoy myself; I just need something to eat.

Henri left.

The Lips left. He invited me to a French punk rock gig and I could hardly wait to see those car bumpers again. The Lips has transformed me. I'm going to have an early night. I'm alone in the studio on the boulevard Saint-Denis.

I'm a small sunflower seed. The bed is the size of a room. When I take a breath, I feel like my body will explode.

Now I'm looking at the stained window. I can recognise all the immense cups and plates on top of the fridge.

I've been laid in the earth: I'm a plant.

Now here comes Ladders opening the window. He says he loves me. I'm pretty sure I don't know what love is. I do know I adore his voice, which makes me feel like a goddess when he's telling me stories and inventing things for us to do.

In his hand, everything is too big. I'm scared. It's me, can't you see that? No – he's filling his pipe with tobacco, and dropping me on top of it.

He's putting the pipe in his mouth. I can see up his nostrils and stubbled face. Now he's pushing me down. Then he lights the pipe with a match and I feel myself dying.

I saw Pierre again, and yes I would like to have a coffee with him this afternoon (any chance of a Croque Monsieur?). He makes me hold my shoulders back and look out of the window. Some things I will never forget from my grandmother. I don't like to talk to him, I feel I'm not saying what I want to hear from myself. I'd like to be in love with him while he painted me on the sofa. I'd like it to show in the painting so that in twenty years' time everyone would say: God, you can tell she really loved him – like Olga in the Picassos.

When my mother used to take me to galleries, I would admire the work and wanted to be one of the models. Arriving in Paris, I thought I could go to a model agency and become a painter's model, get set in Montmartre. The few painters I have met are short and really wrinkly and stink of Gitanes – Serge Gainsbourg with paintbrushes. No offence to Serge, but I was thinking more Modigliani. I want a semi-suicidal genius who's devastatingly handsome in an ugly way. Now this one wants to paint me, Pierre; there's definitely no madness here. I don't want to see him naked.

I have to go. I have to meet Sam, my English scavenging companion. He came up to me and said, 'God, you look as hungry as I feel.' He saw through me, so we have to be friends. Then I'm meeting Inès. She's sneaked into my life – it just happened; after a few coffees we just gelled into place. Inès is so shy, and yet she works as a stripper. She can hardly talk to a man when she's not working. She is my temptress: she offers me work. The men put notes into her bikini slips . . . Burger Kings, Croque Monsieurs, Big Macs.

I want to sit by the café and look sad; and look like I'm thinking . . . Actually I'm thinking about . . . my life so far and how I'd like it to go.

paint
sing
dance
bar
learn French
journal
superglue for nails
travel
my breasts to get bigger so I can wear a string top and they'll look like they'll pop with passion when I see *the* man. Having to share a dormitory with a girl whose breasts defied gravity and who always got the praise from the boys because of her huge tits has marked me. I'd cry because mine just wouldn't grow:

I must, I must, I must improve my bust.
The bigger the better
The stronger the wetter
The boys depend on us.

Basically, the studio that I'm in belongs to a friend of my aunt. He's a record producer (Ludlow – my aunt calls him Ladders). He picked me to be in a Norwegian pop video when I was fifteen. The video deal fell through, and now he wants to seduce me. My aunt has no idea.

Once every two or three weeks, a limo comes to the boulevard Saint-Denis and collects me. I go to the airport to meet him and we spend a weekend together here in Paris, then he glides back to New York. He sleeps on the sofa. We haven't slept together, the Madonna and the whore scenario is rooted in his head. My grandmother was so right about this. He talks about blues music and about a future for us. He asked me to be his mistress and I thought, I've read about this, it's what people used to do in the olden days, and it's got to be done once in my life. My family, of course, think I'm studying and in love with Paris. The downside is there's no food. I don't want to tell my aunt how mean he is. My allowance from mama keeps getting spent the day it arrives – Sam and I are living off it. I think I can handle this and have a great time too. I immediately understood that this person needs women to be hard on him. He likes the fact that I am indifferent to him as a suitor.

One day I found some lists of his – they make my lists look tame. It's refreshing to seem to be the reasonable rational one sometimes. The drawback is I'm not a kept woman. He keeps this studio empty anyway and there really isn't a scrap of food in this deal, let alone any pocket money. I thought 'mistress' meant everything I wanted was delivered to my door.

Henri got me into his friend's model agency. He wanted me to do it; I wanted to eat. The model agency has shocked me into shape. How much time can be spent waiting for other people? They constantly brush my hair – I hate having my hair brushed: my tangles are sacred. And it's so boring sitting around on recruitment missions. Make-up, more make-up and then under really hot lights. You can't read. There are no snacks around the set, no one eats. The photographer runs around doing something he obviously enjoys; you just sit there . . . The models have been waiting all day to see J.M., the head of the agency whom a few of them had slept with at the summer fashion shows and were hoping for another shot before the spring shows.

Am I a fashion model? No! Well, I hope not for long. The only thing I've been put up for so far is a Mexican beer advert. Like Henri, I don't think his friend is very successful. The agency seems to be sinking.

Ladders asked me to go to Prague with him for a few weeks on a recruitment trip to sign up a Czechoslovakian punk band. I said yes immediately.

Met The Lips at a dance hall and I could tell he liked the way I moved. I didn't want to leave. I find him devastatingly attractive. I think about him so much I've got used to him in my mind. It was rushed and I felt myself let go of him reluctantly. I called him from the studio just to hear his voice.

Called The Lips again, talked for hours. What about? No idea, it's not important right now, but it felt good.

Called The Lips to say goodbye, got his answering machine,

listened twice to remember his voice and bring back what he looked like while I went to Prague.

A smash as the glass from the studio window breaks. A cloak taking me up: it's Batman, only he's black. I don't scream. He hooks himself to the balcony. My legs are wrapped round him. The music starts: Vivaldi's *Four Seasons*. We're humming to it. I feel sexy. Can you make me fly? I'm flying round the studio with him. Can we fuck while we fly? No. Gravity problems. OK, on to the floor. Lost the feeling but we do it anyway. I take off his rubber cloak and he's naked underneath. He's got fur like a bat and says that he likes to eat and have sex upside down. While he moans, my face burrowed in his fur, he bites my face and flies out of the window again.

Pigalle to rue Saint-Martin, *en route* to the Alliance française. Am I a student? Well, I look like a student today: satchel, Converse All Star boots, pencils. I'm trying. Most of my classmates are Vietnamese. They don't speak English and they don't really get the French. My other school is the Jacques le Coq School of Mime in the boxing ring where Edith Piaf's husband used to fight. Classes at L'Alliance cross over, the teacher mimes, the Vietnamese struggle with his charades: a book, a film, a play? My aunt only allowed me to come to Paris with Ladders on condition that I continued my education. So far, the French is a bit slow. I'm reading Molière's *The Miser* in English on the Métro. He's making me laugh out loud.

I'm late again, sitting on a bench, it's cold and I haven't had any breakfast. I constantly take notes; I'm always afraid I'll forget things. I have to live the present so intensely because I know I'll forget the past. If I lose it – then there's just now. I can't even remember Brasil. I can't remember my father – I've only heard about him. He was a landowner. He met my mother when he was visiting London and said two words to her. She was nineteen. I've been waiting for a man to say two words to me and I'll follow him. But if they say just two words, the two words are foul, or they say millions of them and none of them seem right.

Lists are a way of holding on to the future. You make your lists and even if something goes wrong, it's like the bones are there. Everywhere round the house I hide them: inside books, behind shelves, under the mattress. Then when I least expect them, they turn up:

    have four kids
    take out split ends
    learn to cook
    read more
    smoke just Gitanes
    get nails covered, superglue if no luck
    learn French
    get some Chinese overalls
    learn to stretch my own canvases
    practice Spanish for the Mexico Circus

I feel good. I feel good a lot. I feel safe. 'How can a woman expect to be happy with a man who treats her as if she were a perfectly rational being.'

I feel good.

If you could see me now,
The one who said she'd never be alone,
The one who said she'd never walk away.

I try to paint. I could have just gone upstairs at home to my mother's studio, and lifted the dust sheets from her easels and palettes and picked up her brushes. I like what she did: canvases with washes of autumn colours and portraits of her friends. Modigliani used to give all his models incredibly long necks; my mother was the opposite. A critic once said she made the whole world look like a breed of toads squashed under a stone. We didn't talk to him again, but he did have a point, because our friends were not actually neckless. They loved my mother despite her tendency to give them all that tortoise look.

I didn't want to go up into her studio, though. I wanted to be like her but at a distance. I have an easel and my mother's overall and lots of respect for my mother's hidden order. I didn't realise paint went hard if you left the lid off the tube, and as to the brushes – they are nearly screwdrivers now. So I paint Inès, over and over. I don't like what comes. I keep feeling I could express something but I express a lot of mess. Maybe this is it. In years to come, will people take it and call it my messy period? I give up for a bit, then every month I try to paint again. It's a private passion: SHE WAS A GREAT PAINTER.

I'd like to write about my childhood, but I change my views on it too much so I'd like to start from Paris in September, aged sixteen after:

a difficult birth
a sweaty country
a god-like, beautiful father
a strong mother who is the A-side of me
travelling around Europe
English boarding school
falling in love with Italy

Because my life could be starting in Paris in September after being born somewhere I know nothing about, to someone I know nothing about and a mother who got hit by a bus and doesn't know if she's coming or going.

I want to become a painter.

And get into a ring with a whip – only in Mexico.

Now I can start my diary. I always thought that when I was sixteen I would shed my childhood, whether it had been a good or a bad childhood. Bits of it still pop out of me, though, at certain times, like sitting on some steps chewing chicken bones with another little kid and sucking bits of skin.

CHAPTER II

Ladders was worried about his packing, but I know how to soothe him. He went on ahead. I packed in minutes. Finished Molière's *The Miser*. There was some kind of festival all over Pigalle. The transvestites had come out of the woodwork. On my first day in Paris I was chased up the street by one I call Follie. She's a Brazilian transvestite who sits in a Range Rover on the rue Saint-Denis outside a rambling beautiful block. The street is full of her friends, but Follie is the youngest of them. She has a huge black and white dog that always sleeps in the back of the car.

Follie has padded hips and stubbled tits in a dirty sequinned top. She has long, knobbly legs with strong calves. Her mouth is so large and long it looks like a Métro station. Her eyes are completely black, there's something in there that makes me look away. Her pimp is short and Calabrian. He manages to use his hands to express his every sentence and hardly ever to let go of her padded ass and his well-padded groin. I think he thinks I'm a transvestite too. When Follie chases me, she says I have something. Is she talking about a hidden dick? I get panicked when I see her on my way to get bread and cigarettes. I put on my trainers and leg it past her jeep. She's fast. Maybe the South American connection is what gets her going. Maybe she just wants to gossip about Salvador de Bahia with someone she imagines has come from there more recently than her/himself. Either way, I'm building up my sprint.

I found out a few days ago why prostitutes often have some front teeth missing – their pimps do it to them so they can still give blow jobs when they're drugged out of their minds.

I've looked inside Follie's Range Rover; when it's rocking I know it's safe to pass. She's customised the seats with fake leopard skin. She's got teddies in all the pockets: Pooh Bear meets the Voodoo Queen. Skulls, claws, family pictures, herbs, human hair and an arsenal of make-up.

Today Follie chased me to the taxi, lifting her tiny skirt up and saying, 'Couchy couchy, come to me.' Like hell! I ran, laughing and crying at the same time. She found it hysterical. But sometimes she just looks sad and smiles through the wound-down blacked-out window. It's as though she were back in the sticky heat of the hill streets of Bahia with the rambling palaces of the slave-traders falling down behind their battered shutters. And the women in the gutters with their coloured bandannas are calling out for customers to buy mangoes and plantains, magic herbs and pussy. By the main square, the cathedral invites her to step into its soothing balm and wander around in the cool embrace of the blue birds on the old Portuguese tiles on the walls.

Follie turns tricks in her Range Rover, dozens a day. I wonder how many thousands of people she's tasted, etc. etc. to get it. Maybe she isn't sad at all, maybe she's exhausted. Yet she still conjures up the energy to chase me.

I feel like a goat in airports. It always feels like me and my luggage are never smart enough and I've packed too much. When I was little, we travelled with so many leather suitcases, canvases, easels and things. Even when they were empty they were really heavy. Whenever we arrived at airports or stations there would be lots of trouser suits and comfortable trainers and we completely stuck out, my mother with her cigarette holders, Spinelli velvet gowns, Tibetan bandaged satin boots, dressed up by my mother, standing out, marked by our luggage. When I look around at other people's luggage, I always feel that somehow I should be different, that I'm not up to scratch. Airports are the only places where I feel I stand out in the wrong way. I have spent thousands of hours studying and practising the art of standing out. I think I might get a Ph.D in it, yet I cannot get a handle on luggage and it's all my mother's fault because she made us travel with such an entourage and such a ridiculous amount of crap that I feel weighed down by it even now, even when it isn't here. I feel it's going to come around the carousel. That it's going to chase me across the check-in desk and hunt down porters, pressganging innocent bystanders into lifting it.

From the time my mother was hit by a bus, she never seemed to know whether she was in the Gare du Nord or the North Pole. She would behave on the Paris Métro as though she were the grande dame of the Trans-Siberian Express. She was always kind of flamboyant before the accident, but she had a firm grip on reality at least for us kids. She held it together, she set up picnics, made up stories, organised gin rummy and endless games of I Spy for Eddie, my big brother. She gave the impression of being carefree, but she actually made us feel safe because we knew she had organised it all.

I can remember quite a lot about what my mother was like before she got blown down the Yellow Brick Road. She used to be obsessed with floors – they'd start off as dark oak and then sand and lime down to a luminous whiteness. For every house we moved to, it wasn't the pictures or the walls that worried her, it was the floors. She'd be up at night after we'd gone to bed, sanding. No one was allowed to help.

She collected antique clothes which she used to lug around in her trunks. Everywhere we settled, she'd tip these trunks out (to her lover's despair) and they'd heap up with velvets and silks, cuffs of embroidery, kimonos, Chinese coats from Xian, braids and beads and 1920s sequins. In hotels, the chambermaid would sometimes report a burglary and my mother would then have to explain that it was just her way to jumble her clothes as though the room had been rifled by vandals. My mother never touched any fabric that wasn't beautiful.

She didn't drive. When we rented apartments, we had to carry in our shopping, which I hated. Everywhere apart from her dressing room was always tidy, clean, and full of vases of fresh flowers.

She spent a lot of time in her studio, painting in her huge overalls which were too big for her with their one pocket caked in paint where she wiped her brushes. She always wore an obi – a kimono sash – to keep her overalls fastened. No matter how busy she was, she always had time for me. She gave me a huge confidence and a sense of such safety that for years after she was knocked down in Birmingham New Street I just refused to believe that she wouldn't one day be herself again and come back to me and Eddie.

During the months, first in intensive care and then at St Thomas's hospital, Cinzia, our Italian nanny, who had been with us since Eddie's birth, picked up the pieces. Afterwards, when my mother returned, she was back with us but it was as though she wasn't really there. She has never been the same since. Cinzia has kept everything running as before, but she is now my mother's nanny and all Eddie and I have is a maternal shell and whatever memories of what she was like before she set off for a stroll in Birmingham having missed her connection to London after a day at a friend's gallery opening.

My grandmother used to say 'live each day as your last', and she used to say 'always wear clean underclothes as you never know when you could get hit by a bus'. Every day that my mother dressed me, she used to repeat this as she pulled up my Italian underpants (ironed by Cinzia).

It was the only small bonus of her hit-and-run accident that on that day in Birmingham, my mother's underpants were not only clean, they were La Perla and of the finest oyster silk.

PRAGUE, OCTOBER 20TH

In the first-class cabin the air hostess keeps waking me up to chat, but really to find out if I'm Ladders's mistress or his daughter. She seems genuinely concerned, maybe she's planning to send me back as an unaccompanied minor to my family.

There is fog in Prague so we can't land there. We have to go and wait like sheep somewhere else until they bother to tell us what is happening.

Inside the waiting area two young guys who've been diverted for hours suss me out to see if they can come up and chat me up, as all the other girls seem to have already had a going over. Ladders is asleep. There is only one man who looks like my kind of thing: intellectual, artistic, a bit rough, shy, almost the package. We smile at each other, then he leaves. How perfect, we're not going to see each other again. Inès says that's best, then you don't get to find out the nasty bits.

On the telly, sixties working girls do exercises. It's nice not to understand what anybody's talking about and have the excuse of a foreign language.

Five gin and tonics later (none of which I drank), we took a train to Prague. I'd wanted to rent a car or a motorbike to get there with me as driver, but Ladders was too practical and I am too young. I hate not being old enough to drive legally.

Ladders likes to carry everything in a ridiculous tartan rucksack.

The train is 1950s, zinc. It is dark and I am behind the Iron Curtain.

I pretended I was on the Trans-Siberian Express and wandered along the corridor. I smoked a black Sobranie with some American kids. I went back to our compartment dizzy and ready for anything. I stripped to the waist and woke Ladders up, thinking this would be the perfect time to lose my virginity. It felt too in the open. The fat inspector caught me with my shirt off. They have their own keys. I wasn't ready anyway, just bored.

Ladders is here for his record company signing up a new Czechoslovakian punk band and to 'jam as much culture and other remarkable things into me as possible'. I called The Lips and listened to his waking-up voice. I can't remember what he looks like. I'm not going to think about you for two weeks.

My hot flush is back again. I'm told I should take a sip of alcohol when things go blurry and warm. But I like the time out I get with these rushes that make me go so cosy inside, like inside a huge bearskin rug. I hope when I fall in love it feels like this. I think I'll buy a silver flask with my initials on it.

I thought about what would be nice for the studio. I slept well: no sweaty strange dreams. My head feels too clear.

Last night, I watched Ladders asleep on the train. I couldn't sleep as I kept getting urges to be near someone.

If you could hear me now
Singing somewhere in the lonely night

What is it that makes people be together? My aunt, for instance, wanted to be like Amy Johnson and fly round the world, to which end she had a great collection of flying jackets and got a job for a few months at a travel agency which is where she met my uncle.

Singlehandedly she managed to screw up his entire itinerary in such a spectacular way that he went all the way back to the Fulham Road to find her and demand an explanation. That evening, they had their first date. They've been together ever since.

My grandmother told me she was relieved to have my mother off her hands as she hadn't believed that anyone would have had the staying power to keep up with her drift. My dad won my mother with two words – South America – even though that was really all he could say. They stayed together for nearly ten years and then he died.

Being together feels strange as an idea because we do so much to be ourselves, to find ourselves. Giving yourself for life to somebody else while still trying to find yourself is weird. You suddenly meet somebody and you become coupled to them, you almost become a part of that person. Other people perceive you through this other person. You get joint presents and discounts on holidays. Are we really drawn to these people or do we get to a point of disillusionment or peer pressure when we think, sod it, I'll take so and so? And for a man, is it really like whipping his dick out on a roulette table and throwing the dice with his friends blowing on them for luck?

When I meet the man for me, if there is one, I hope it'll be without any bullshit, any discussion, any complications or lies. I want to make eye contact and feel 'Oops, this is it' and when the train stops we both get off at the same stop and are together for ever after. I would have liked it to have been on a bus in Morocco, but since my mother was knocked down by a bus, I've had to change the dream and make it a train.

I want to look after somebody. I want my love to be my greatest achievement.

As I've realised through this relationship with Ladders, this isn't the big one. I know it's not. I can spend time with him or with someone else, but I want to spend a lot of time not with him, alone in my fantasy, waiting for the right one to come along. Sometimes you can walk into the shell of a relationship while waiting for something else. I think there's going to be a lot of that.

Everything in Prague seems grey, the people are pale and the city smells of boiled cabbage. But the people have a funny way of being which makes me feel good.

I think I look good on trains: the light is good.

I am reading *Cousine Bette*.

Everything here is so cheap, and I have money. I think of the song of Francis blah blah blah I heard in The Lips's house: a dollar goes a long way here.

Cinzia would like me to marry a Venetian count. My aunt wants me to have a nice boyfriend of my own age. They both think that Ladders is the perfect gentleman and they are happy he has let me use his studio and that he's never there. I really can't bring myself to explain the complexities of this situation. As Inès says, 'No sex, no food'.

My tits ache and I'm still growing. I can feel it in the back of my legs and in my breasts. I think that is why Ladders likes me. When his friends ask how I am, he can say, 'Still growing'.

When I'm seventeen I think things will be completely different. Who will be burrowing into my heart and life then?

Theatre is something I would love to be involved in. But I don't want to make my life come out of a play. Everybody takes their life as they are moved by it. Love's not ruled by reason – I like to believe that. I'd like to believe that I'm going to be a great actress, but frankly, it is not going to happen. The nearest I've got to a theatre is my two lines in *Daisy Pulls It Off* at school.

The night travel has made my voice low and I feel sexy and continental. I called Cinzia in Italy – she thinks it sounds like a sore throat.

More bad news about the San Francisco earthquake: over 273 dead. It's just too many numbers. God, one person you know goes and you can't even get around that.

I learned that a misanthrope is someone who doesn't like people and that a misogynist is someone who doesn't like women. I don't like one or the other at times. If I imagine 273 girls at a school assembly, then it begins to sink in and I can try to imagine their fear and the smothering.

I want to write to all the people I can write to:

my mother
Cinzia
my aunt

Eddie in New York
Chiara – my Italian girlfriend
Sofia – Italian girlfriend
Santino – my neighbour in Italy, my age
Sam – my Paris friend

Hey, The Lips, let's go for a swim while the water is cool and get that tingly feeling while we are still friends.

I wonder if my taste in men is good. It seems right when I see it. But I see *its* quite often, in a voice, or eyes etc. Which just shows they are not the right one.

As time goes by, with what my grandmother would have described as 'monotonous regularity', a lot of men have reached that moment when they offer their bodies completely, which is the last thing I want. Actually, not everyone, because there was a wellington-boot salesman on the Riviera whom I visited for months in his shop. I used to watch him dressing and undressing the shop dummies in fishing gear. He hardly spoke, so that was intriguing, and he radiated a heat that I felt connected to. He had black curly hair and blue eyes. After hours, we spent a lot of time huddled in cafés, and that was it. Nothing happened. He never made a pass, which excited me to distraction.

I took matters into my own hands and hatched a plan with my cousins who were spending the summer with us. I turned up at his apartment in tennis shoes, naked under my raincoat, drenched by the electric storm that was bouncing off the sea. I felt ready to lose my virginity. I had tried to funnel that message into his brain from my journey through the rain. When he answered the door, he looked very red and flustered. I could feel the intense warmth from his body and I assumed it was for me and I assumed his manhood pushed against his sarong was for me too. I opened my coat before he could speak and threw myself into his arms. Over his shoulder, another flustered, naked man was standing in a doorway asking how long he was going to be.

How can I put that feeling into words? Even into my diary it is not coming. It is one of the few things that has ever left me speechless. Let's just say that it still took me some time to understand the full extent of the situation.

    numb
    grief
    revenge
    death
    anger
    outrage
    want to be a nun
    hate wellington boots

OCTOBER 21ST

I dreamt about being in the war and being a peasant girl in a camp.

Everything that is old and beautiful is being destroyed. They want only the young to live. I have two children and have to choose between one or the other. A guard tells me that I'm special and I can survive this. So he picks up my baby girl with her curly blonde hair which he rubs bald against his hard uniform.

Then everything is cold and modern and I am a German. I am in uniform. There are soldiers, tanks and guns. I have killed three people and my lover has had to go and fight: `Goodbye, my darling, until the next world.'

I want to wake up and leave all this.

`Down on the floor! Watch this, little girl, your mamma is going to start begging soon.'

There are sixteen soldiers all with their dicks hanging out of their perfect uniforms.

My baby is screaming for them to stop.

`It's only a game.' He smiles at me. Then I faint. I faint and wake up in a hospital. I'm crazy from the things they've done, the voices of the soldiers and my baby's screams.

I meet Hitler and he drags me off the street. Yes, I can soothe him. When I wipe his sweaty forehead, he falls asleep. I won't kill him yet. He has to just press himself against me and a damp stain appears on his grey uniform.

He gives me a bubble car to drive around in. He lies in the back of the car. He wants vegetables. They have to be fresh. Yes, I detest him. He's a soothable person. I know I'm going to kill him. I'm nearly ready.

Prague looks a bit like Edinburgh. I like the cold weather with sun shining. In the Lux, old alcoholics take their first *vin rouge* while I take an orange juice, watching their red eyes and yellow fingers.

Postcard time.

Dear Cinzia,

I'm in the Austro-Hungarian Empire. I think I'm witnessing something before a change. There is every shade of grey – charcoal, slate, lead, smoke and ash embraced by sunlight.

I embrace you,
Una

Dear Chiara,

I'm in the Austro-Hungarian Empire. I think I'm witnessing something before a change.

There is every shade of grey – charcoal, slate, ash, smoke and lead embraced by sunlight.

I embrace you,
love, Una

Dear Sam,

I'm in the Austrian–Hungarian Empire. I think I'm witnessing . . .

My mother taught me to use big handwriting on postcards and appear to jam them full when really you'd hardly said anything and to make sure the last bit spilled into the margin.

Our hotel is Renaissance and it's stunning. We have a modern suite that overlooks dirty wooden terraces and little flats with lovely Gothic stained-glass windows covered in smut.

I've been wondering about reincarnation: everyone I know who believes in it seems to have been something exotic and wonderful in their previous lives. No one I know seems to have been a one-armed beggar in a filthy back street, or a fifties housewife with an abusive husband. When I ask them about this, they get annoyed. But if so many people's lives were dull, where have all their spirits gone? And why have so many bores been handmaidens to Cleopatra, Barbary pirates or burned as witches? What about the workers?

The flowery art nouveau lounge is peppered with loud, flat-faced Germans. The hotel has a wonderful marble staircase. There was a marble staircase in the house I grew up in in Brasil. It was malachite-green and accidents happened on it. I've heard about them second hand, mostly from Eddie. My childhood is like a jumble sale – a heap of things and labels which I rummage through and just pick out the bits that interest me. Like the man who married his donkey on the coffee plantation where I was born. Or my cousin who could never decide whether to get out of bed or not. I keep my energy level on a permanent high in case one day I wake up like him and literally can't get out of bed. He used to get stuck there trying to decide whether to get up now or later, now or later, and whole days went by like that. I know where he's coming from. I have his blood in my veins. I'm the last of a line of inbreeds.

*　　*　　*

Ladders has to stay with his band here all day and I meet him at the corner of Wenceslas Square each night.

Today I walked around the centre of Prague and got so lost. It has cobbled streets and frescoed façades in a mixture of Venice, Italian towns and Austria. Alleyways lead into spacious squares.

The bridges are blocked with the abandoned Skodas of people trying to flee to the West. Something is on the brink of changing here. It's in the air. They've had enough.

All over the city, people have abandoned their cars as though a nuclear fallout had just occurred. Some streets were deserted, blocked. In others, lots of people carried bags and bundles and babies with them and they were hurrying away.

I noticed it most on the bridge because I was crossing in a taxi just as a traffic jam closed around us and we were stuck in the middle of deserted Skodas whose drivers had literally just skipped off the bridge and were scrambling over the fence of the German Embassy. Eventually, we had to reverse off the bridge.

If I come back a year from now, I wonder what I'll see. This feels like a city about to re-create itself, and yet life goes on: kids go to school, most people go to work, bars open. I think this greyness is on the way out.

Last night we found a dungeon beer bar. I sat and smoked a calabash pipe with Czech tobacco while Ladders got totally plastered. I went to the loo and watched a man in a wheelchair reversing into a tin hat box.

OCTOBER 27TH

This is my first city with trams.

I looked at the shop windows with nothing in them but piles of tins.

Now I can buy things there's nothing to buy. I want:

shampoo
an English–Czech phrase book
an antique clock
a 30s watch
tight, pencil skirt
presents for Italy
presents for Paris
something for Eddie
dangly amber earrings
a calabash pipe

OCTOBER 28TH

I went with Ladders and his band to a restaurant with 1900s decor and got hissed at for smoking before eight-thirty. I guess punk is punk in any country, but I kept expecting rats to crawl out of any one of the band's pockets. These people are *heavy*!

Supper. Guess what I had? Boiled cabbage, boiled potatoes and boiled meat. I ate like I enjoyed it, but every day, twice a day I eat boiled cabbage, boiled potatoes etc. It's always the same and mountains of it. I suppose I shouldn't complain – at least it's food. Outside, the crowds are surging, heading *en masse* towards the embassies, towards the frontier, straining at their Russian leash.

Even in the most expensive restaurant in Prague, the menu was the same. It cost $2.20 for eight people – nearly a week's wage to a factory worker.

I tried to make eye-contact for a lot of the night with a cross-eyed young boy. I'm in a 1950s black and white movie and I wear my hair up.

OCTOBER 29TH

My mother's birthday. Try all day to send flowers. Feel upset even though I know she won't know it is her birthday. But she notices flowers. Slept early with raincheck on the cabbage.

OCTOBER 30TH

Brassica time. The men and women wear seventies jeans and hair-cuts. I find myself gagging to get my hands on the women at the next table. Just a tiny make-over – a little bit of colour on the cheeks, though after a few days here, the cabbage is whitening my skin too.

My crepe 1920s gown caused a sensation, but not quite the one I'd dreamt of creating back in Paris. Maybe it was because I was barefoot.

ROMEO,

ROMEO!

WHEREFORE ART THOU

ROMEO?

'Ah, there you are, Mr Johnson, you can take your thumb out of my ass now.'

CHAPTER III

The chambermaid came to service our room while I was still in bed. It's not the usual woman, it's a girl my age. I can't manage to communicate to her to come back later. I feel very uncomfortable. My first reaction is to start tidying up myself. My second reaction is anxiety. I have a complex about being taken for a hispanic maid. I think it started in a hotel in Milan when I'd bought a fifties pinafore that charladies wear and adapted it, I thought, fabulously. I was caught down a corridor by a Roman lady who informed me that I could now clean her room. I was too mortified to say I was a guest, and it's stuck with me.

Even Ladders asked me to put on a little frilly apron and high heels to bring him breakfast in bed once. He scripted me to say, 'Señor, your coffee is ready' in a nasal Spanish accent. I liked the dressing up bit, but I did it with a shit-eating grin, hoping the coffee would choke him.

If God exists and he had been nailed to the cross, revenge would have a big space on his agenda.

In the olden days, when people worshipped the sun, there was a point: their crops didn't grow without it.

I've grown up around Catholicism and I see it rooted in fear. All that gold in the Vatican Museum is amazing but I have a strong feeling it's wrong. The Pope seems much more of a nice guy in Italy where not many people take any notice of him and condoms are for sale at most sweet counters. In Brasil, we think he's the mouthpiece of God and we do exactly what he says, as in have dozens of children and starve. Have you seen São Paulo?

It would be great to believe that there was somebody who'd protect you and care for you. A supreme being who'd stop you being run over by a double-decker.

I tried praying once, when my grandmother was ill. She had cancer. I tried and she died a slow and horrible death.

My aunt is always saying 'this is not a rehearsal'. But all my life has been a second chance, a lucky break, and I know it. I died when I was a baby and was resuscitated in hospital.

NOVEMBER 3RD

What is the difference between love and infatuation?

I don't feel as though I've ever been in love, but I want to be, I think I do. I've still got to lose my virginity.

Infatuations:

Giorgio – who delivered huge cranes to my mother's house when she had some work done
Alessandro – my first dizzy spells
Matteo – the wellington-boot seller

Massimo – I met him only once at a dinner party. What a twinkle!

The Lips

To be able to feel a warm kiss from the man I love keeps me awake – hot and dizzy. Anna Magnani in her slips in the cramped apartments in Rome, her hair back-combed, the shadows under her eyes – I want those sleepless nights.

Thank God for flirting. I'm maintaining my thing with Ladders with it. It's the part I enjoy. I will fulfil a lot of fantasy roles for him if it means no sex, no snogging. I feel like a book by Anaïs Nin, endless titillation and erotic fantasies at a distance.

I've always been tactile, I am with my family and friends, so the hugs and the handholding that Ladders no doubt sees as a step towards the rosebud are actually meaningless.

People say it doesn't show when you lose your virginity, but I hope I'm going to look a little bit different when I lose mine.

Can you be infatuated with two people at the same time? Right now though, it's The Lips. He told me that the first moment he saw me he had a flash – a vision – and he was dumbstruck and heartstruck. He wanted me to be the mother of his children and for us to get married when I was older.

Do I fit into this? Why couldn't he just say, 'Fancy some pasta?' or 'a day at the beach?' It seems that men constantly project their fantasies on to us. It's as though I'm a screen at a cinema. I know that I fantasise a lot, but I do it on a blank screen, I want to be on my own when I'm dreaming, I don't need to drag anyone else into it.

NOVEMBER 4TH
'The world and I are on excellent terms.'

Reading Oscar Wilde had given me a huge confidence in my future romance. I suddenly understand about strangers. It is so obvious that the reason I haven't met *The Man* is because he's a stranger. Like my father was to my mother. One day, he'll just turn up. Meanwhile, I have never heard of him. This is the missing link in the chain: 'The man must be quite respectable, one has never heard his name before in the whole course of one's life, which speaks volumes for a man nowadays.'

I'm in a dark alleyway off Wenceslas Square.

Suddenly it's wet and I'm crawling along metal streets which get tighter and tighter. I am inside an old radiator going up and down the rusty ridges. At one end there is a bucket of boiled cabbage, at the other, a pop singer in tight lavender lurex trousers is singing my name, 'Una, Una,' and beckoning to me to come on stage. I crawl up to the microphone with strands of sauerkraut in my hair. I sing backing. It is a Czech love song which involves a lot of head swaying.

Through the smoke I can hardly see anyone in the audience. The show is a flop.

My head lolls from side to side and then drops off. Someone from the audience steps up and puts it in his top pocket. Where my head was grows a cabbage with a face exactly like the singer. I have frizzy blonde hair and a receding chin.

Ladders is out tonight on business and I'm alone *again*.

One night, after a dinner at The Lips's house in Paris – a mews house full of princely things – we were very formal when we parted.

At the car I told Inès I'd be right back and I went to talk to him. He was surprised to see me again. I told him I needed him to know that he was sometimes on my mind, that I was leaving for Prague and I didn't want him digging into my brain. He told me things I already knew about how he felt. Then I felt uncluttered and I liked how that felt.

I've decided to live in Paris for a while and give the Alliance française another chance. I'm going to

paint
learn Russian
dance the tango
make a garden on the studio roof
stop biting my nails
teach English to Henri's daughter
photograph the girls at work
bleach moustache

I have made a list of people I know in alphabetical order. I need to meet an X, a B and an N. I'm reading *Women in their Married Bliss* by Edna O'Brien – it's understandable and down to the point. Sometimes I think of myself as Irish with very red cheeks and freckles and a perfect skin with my sleeves rolled up, making soda bread surrounded by cows and crucifixes.

NOVEMBER 5TH

A penny for the Guy?

I went to a concert of classical music in a Gothic church. I listened with my eyes closed but I wanted someone to lean on and snug up to. Ladders picked me up after the concert and we tried a different restaurant. The menu was like herpes, it came with us.

Ladders entertained his band over dinner. I waltzed with the cook all through the night until it was time to go. I was taught to waltz by an Italian police captain, a Tuscan maresciallo who had once been a ballroom dancer. I met him on my fourteenth birthday after I had had a crash on my Vespa. They said I had punctured my spleen. When I came-to in hospital the Maresciallo was standing over me, trying to comfort me.

I wanted my mother to be there for me. I had her presence and armfuls of flowers from her pots and that was all. She never showed how much or how little she understood about anything. There was a vagueness, a void around her. Cinzia was scared at what her reaction might have been. This was the first time she had been near a hospital since her own accident. But not even the hospital clicked a response. She filled my room with the scent of orange flowers and she gazed out of the window, I think at the hospital garden. From time to time she mumbled, 'That's lovely, my darling.'

I never really write about Cinzia and that's because she seems so much a part of everything I do and am. She has a tic on her right eye, a photograph of her dead husband in a locket and a lovely smell.

Cinzia called Eddie over to be with me, and it was great to see him, but I wanted my mother too.

The Maresciallo always brought a bunch of grapes, and after a bit, he used to want to waltz. He'd take his gun out of his holster and put it on our kitchen dresser, and then we'd dance. He was about five foot one, and he used to say it didn't matter how tall a man was when he danced. (Does this sound like a short person's comment?) He'd put his thumb in the small of my back to control my movements. He could virtually paralyse a woman on this pressure point: one false step and you were a rag doll.

I watched an old Czech couple dancing. They were in bliss and he kept winking at her and whispering things in her ear that made her laugh. It made me cry, the thought of two people loving each other for their whole lives, growing old together and still flirting and laughing, achieving a life together to give love a reason and not just to be a series of empty loveless years.

Later, I tried to sleep and felt very alone; I lay awake scared.

CHAPTER IV

I am Jeanne Moreau in *Jules et Jim*, and I am Anna Magnani. I am Cat Ballou. I'm a wild woman living on my own ranch, people fear me but are intrigued by me. I have a strong past I never talk about. I'm Modigliani's model and lover – but not the one who threw herself out of the window when she was pregnant. I am a peasant's daughter in the south of Italy who falls in love and my family forbid me the marriage. They send me to a convent, but my lover comes and rescues me when I am about thirty and mad with religion. I'm an heiress and I buy a small island in the Caribbean, I adopt nine children at a time like my great-grandmother in Belém and bring them up only to adopt another nine. I'm a revolutionary who doesn't really understand it at all at the beginning, but then I get swallowed up by the cause. It takes up most of my life, secretly, and I can never confide in my family and friends.

When I was a little girl I fantasised too, a lot. If I'd stayed on the fazenda in Bahia where I was born, I'd have fitted in. Everyone there tells stories and embellishes their lives. Growing up in Europe, it took some years to get into the swing of things. I used to think how sad to have to limit your world to just what you can see.

When my grandmother died, I went away to Nevis to spend a month with my godfather. I was nine, and it was my first trip to the tropics since I'd left Brasil four years before. I got some sea urchin spines embedded in my leg. My godfather had scars on his leg where he had been attacked by a shark. It was completely natural to me when I returned to my boarding school to blend these two events.

The girls were really impressed by my scars. They had never been to the Caribbean, but most of them had seen *Jaws*. The story snowballed a little bit further than I had intended and came to a showdown with my headmistress. I stood by my shark, she called in my mother who loyally came up with a very tiny baby shark to back up my lies and save me from losing face. She also took that opportunity to explain the difference between inventing stories and believing them myself. Although I try to be honest with myself, I wouldn't give up daydreaming.

So it wasn't too hard to get into Ladders's bubble when he woke me up in our hotel room to have an in-depth discussion about whether or not I was pregnant by him. He questioned me closely about my periods, about dates, the state of my nipples etc. I didn't bother to point out that I was still a virgin. There was no chance – he had raced ahead to nursery furniture and the pushchair versus pram debate. Things were very strained at the studio. So I just made him some tea.

Wildcat Sally looking mighty pale
sitting by his sweetheart's side
and when his sweetheart said

'Come on let's settle down'
Wildcat raised his head and cried
'Just turn me loose . . .
Don't fence me in!'

Another day of coffee houses. My voice goes really high-pitched and pathetic when I try to explain myself here. I'm speaking in English, Italian, a bit of French, Portuguese but frankly not any Czech and I feel I am making a complete fool of myself. My few lessons at the Jacques le Coq have not helped me here so I end up talking really slowly or not at all. I've decided that I want to get two black and white Neapolitan mastiffs. But I'll have to wait. I can't afford to feed myself yet, let alone two beasts the size of lions.

I feel strange. I'm looking forward to being back in Paris, to being at the studio and planning my days. My stomach had shrunk in the month in Paris. I've been bingeing here. The cabbage is winning. Thank God for my stash of chocolates.

Harry Crosby was one of the richest men in America in the 1920s. He shot himself and his lover in the head after having sex. I wonder if they planned it a long time before they did it?

It would be nice to have freckles and moles all over my body.

NOVEMBER 9TH

I covered my whole body with big and little dots with my felt-tip pen. They looked quite like freckles. But when I came down for dinner, I looked in a permanent state of embarrassment from having scrubbed at them.

I haven't seen any transvestites here, or prostitutes, which is strange because Prague cannot be the only city in the world without any. Ladders says they work as maids and desk clerks in hotels and restaurants. Maybe.

Finally, we went to a game restaurant above Prague. Milos Forman eats here. Of course he eats here, it's the only place you don't have to eat boiled cabbage. It looked like a seedy nightclub set into the mountain from the outside; the inside was stuffed with stuffed game. It was like eating inside a taxidermist's studio. Ladders had a tusk touching the back of his head throughout the meal. We ate and ate and ate and I didn't care about whole families of animals looking down on us with their glass eyes.

I saw a father and daughter idling together and I felt jealous and teary. My father died when I was five. I don't remember him – it's strange you can miss what you don't know. He came from an old family outside Bahia. He played football badly, and tennis very well; he built an electrical dynamo. He was an anglophile and a dog-lover. More importantly he was my dad.

I can fit in in most places, my mother made sure of that. She'd up and move and move us with her without any notice. I used to have to start new schools mid-term in whatever language happened to go with her current destination. This didn't happen to Eddie because he was a lot older, which was just as well because Eddie is shy whereas for me it was a challenge and, mostly, it was fun.

I don't remember the fazenda in Bahia, but sometimes, if confronted with a plate of feijoada, a nice kind of nostalgia comes over me.

When my father had a heart attack on the tennis court behind our house my mother took us to Italy.

NOVEMBER 11TH

In the hotel there are cameras watching at all times. Each time I pass one, I mouth 'He's a spy' over Ladders's head.

I had my breakfast in bed again, then a large glass of warm water, then down on the hideous carpet for the exercises:

stretch to the ceiling
12 touch toes
12 dog position
12 patting under the chin
12 twisting ribs
40 jogging on the spot

I'm not going to do this again.

In the hotel they change everything but the sheets.

Only two cigarettes a day.

The juke box at reception sounds out Chuck Berry.

Today I didn't leave the hotel except to buy some men's vests.

Ladders read to me last night which made me feel closer to him than I ever have. It was a sonnet, fourteen lines, ending:

like

cow

spike

now

Number two is my favourite:

When forty winters shall besiege thy brow
And dig deep trenches in thy beauty's field,
Thy youth's proud livery, so gazed on now,
Will be a tattered weed of small worth held:
Then being asked where all thy beauty lies,
Where all the treasure of thy lusty days,
To say, within thine own deep-sunken eyes,
Were an ill-eating shame and thriftless praise.
How much more praise deserved thy beauty's use,
If thou couldst answer 'This fair child of mine
Shall sum my count and make my old excuse,'
Proving his beauty by succession thine!
    This were to be new made when thou art old,
    And see thy blood warm when thou feelest it cold.

NOVEMBER 12TH

I watched two pigeons on the wooden terraces across the way in serious foreplay. Well, she didn't want it. He had a tiny hard blue willy, which he just kept pushing around in front of her – she didn't seem impressed or moved by this at all.

Inès and I are being offered coffee by a petite women who looks like she owns a boutique, but she doesn't, she has a catalogue of photographs of men. All of them are in three different outfits, casual, smart and naked. Underneath the photos, captions give their names, vital statistics and hobbies. The petite woman leaves us alone to look through the books. Inès chooses a guy called Jacques. Apart from a too strong neck and jaw bone, he's OK. He has amazing eyes, indigo. As I leave the room, Inès is shoving cash into the petite woman's hand which gets bigger and bigger the more francs she clutches.

Next evening I'm at my favourite local restaurant. I haven't been here very often but the waiter greets me warmly. I'm not wearing any pants. Jacques arrives and joins me, his strong hands grip my knees under the table. He senses that no words are appropriate. A fabulous meal and four videos later dawn is breaking and we still haven't had the sex Inès paid for. Jacques tells me his plan to get out of the business. He wants to start up a motorcycle shop in Lyon where he has family. He tells me he drifted into the business because he was broke and hung like a donkey. The video screen goes grey and grainy, blurred images of Jacques' seemingly endless penis glide across the screen.

I woke up and called Inès who told me she had enrolled on a course to teach kindergarten.

I went out with my toothbrush in my hair.

I would like to buy myself lots of nice things when I get back to

Paris and London – unfortunately I have no money but . . .

kimonos – long and short
ballet pumps
cigarette box
seamed stockings
War and Peace
The Brothers Karamazov
an Indonesian puppet
Moroccan lamp
a whole stack of fresh beetroot for my cheeks
a topaz ring 3cm fat
Chinese slippers – red and black
cut-glass wine decanter

I thought I'd never forget Paris yet actually it's fading now. It seems like such a long time ago.

I walked across Wenceslas Square. It was so cold I wrapped my head in my scarf. There was a celebration of the Republic (the public vote and there is no king). It was like *The Unbearable Lightness of Being*, they had tanks on alert like in the film when the Russians invaded Czechoslovakia in the square.

November 15th

Dream dream dream. I spend a lot of my time sleeping now. I have a cold and I don't know how much more cabbage I can cope with, or how many more hours of in-depth intellectual discussions I can sit through. It all seems so depressed that even being happy is a grim and desperate affair often ending in the same Russian song, which I'm told is about going off to war. The settings for our merriment are dungeons; the seats, hard pews and you're just supposed to whack your way through litres of dark beer.

Today we are to be kicked out of the Hôtel de Paris.

I dreamt about being in love in the time of Shakespeare and speaking naturally in thee and thou, and being serenaded.

At reception there is a fuss about the bill, a third of which is my secret phone calls to Italy and Paris. I feel like a complete jerk. Like at school, I fight the accusations to the bitter end, it is my first encounter with itemised phone bills, they list the numbers: my home number, Inès etc.

We are not talking.

We make up a little over a magazine quiz. Apparently, I love myself twenty-five per cent. Ladders, apparently, loves himself seventy-eight per cent.

I want to go to the States soon, buy an old car and cross America without any plans. I can't wait. Well, I have to, not being able to drive or enter bars for another five years.

His tender heir might bear his memory:
But thou, contracted to thine own bright eyes,
Feedest thy light's flame with self-substantial fuel,
Making a famine where abundance lies . . .

During our tiff over my phone bill, I remembered all the names of my infatuations.

I am determined to be honest with myself about this. So, actually, my list should have read:

Antonio
Giorgio
Alessandro
Daniele
Matteo
Davide
Massimo
The Lips

I found out what water sports are – I thought they were people who were remarkably fit and found time to do water-skiing and scuba-diving etc. Pissing on people is really weird. I wonder if it starts by accident?

Molière died on stage during *The Hypochondriac*.
I'm reading William Butler Yeats (Irish, dead).
I went to a sweet cruck-handed doctor, people in the surgery had to take off their shoes. I had to take off my trousers too. He mumbled some remedies for my pain. I'd swap an opal for a kidney stone any day. One of the great things about Jeanne Moreau is that she makes dark shadows under her eyes so sexy. È STUPENDA. Today, with my kidney stones, I've been trying to make my dark under my eyes a

make-up statement but it's not really happening. I'll have to go for the lighter look. If I do it in a not too well-lit room, I end up with whitish streaks round my eyes.

It's probably just as well that tonight I'm going to the circus. I made Ladders pull a lot of strings to get the tickets. It was in a marquee on the outskirts of town, lit by hundreds of torch flames. It was one big family. The audience was ecstatic, and it wasn't put on. It was lovely to see the depression lift for the first time in nearly a month. The women used their long shiny hair to slide down the rope, after a balancing act that made the palms of my hands sweat. Everything was done with such grace, except the animal acts which were a bit sickening to watch. In the last act the bears were dressed in lingerie and trapezed across the marquee.

Three delicious slabs of chocolate cake without actually being sick.

NOVEMBER 16TH

We're spending the night with some friends of Ladders. He says it will be more fun, I think he means we have no hotel to go to. I had an early night and took their kids' top bunk and dreamt of boarding school, sleeping with four bunks to a dormitory, and how Lucy was caught in the broom cupboard trying to have sex with the broom and that was why the dorms were so dirty. And about stupid things like the science teacher, and making him leave the school because we gave him such a hard time. There was a golf course at the end of our grounds where we'd lift up our skirts to the golfers as they were about to putt to distract them from a safe distance. Three hundred and fifty girls closed away from male presence. It was a man obsession, flirting with anything that was male and moved – the deaf gardener and, like a ray of light, a part-time Spanish teacher. There was such a rush to register for his classes that I was too late, so I only ever heard about them secondhand. A lot of our free time was spent looking at a poster of King Dong that a Polish girl in my dorm had managed to smuggle in. King Dong was a porn star, six foot five, black and hung like a stallion. Subsequently . . .

It's been hard not to compare.

CHAPTER V

We walked through the ghetto to see the Jewish cemetery. It's one of the strangest and most beautiful places I've ever been to. There are hundreds of hacked-at stones, some on top of each other going up the hill with their Hebrew inscriptions. The cemetery is overlooked by willows. Rabbi Law's house is a small Gothic building from 1600 which has been made into a museum of pictures done by the children in the concentration camps here in Czechoslovakia. Thirty-five thousand children died in three years. These pictures and stories were the life they thought they could have. Now, years later, me and thousands of tourists, mostly Germans, come and look at them. These graves are scattered with white stones. There are remembrance prayers and notes to the dead.

I'm feeling drained and I don't want to write for a while.

PARIS, NOVEMBER 20TH

This morning Ladders wanted to show me that he could do seventy-five press-ups, which he managed, but he also ended up with a flushed reddish suntan look for the rest of the day. I walked him to the recording studio. I wonder if that's how you look after a night of passion.

Ever since we went to Prague, I've been picking up stray bits of money left round the room or in the pockets of the jackets etc. that I kept borrowing out there, supposedly to keep out the bitter wind, but actually to get a bit of cash. After such a long time, I should have been quite well off, but Ladders is so tight-fisted, it has been an uphill slog. However, I did have a bundle of notes which I took to a bureau de change to convert instantly into yummy French food.

Bad news, Czech money is hardly worth anything.

Good news, there is just enough to keep me for today.

foie gras
Camembert
Brie
canard aux poivres
poulet pimenté à la mode du Nord
bouillabaisse
crème brûlée
lemon sorbet
quiche
croissant
pain au chocolat
boeuf bourguignon
madeleines
moules
omelette farcie

Of the above list of my favourite things I can afford the croissant and the pain au chocolat.

My white vests make my breasts stand out.

All the leaves from the plane trees are blowing and swirling along the pavement, it feels as though they are trying to wrap themselves over my shins. After the greys of Prague, it feels heady to be surrounded by yellows and browns and reds. A Scotsman ahead of me has had leaves blown up his kilt and it is ballooning out.

The Scots were taken to America as indentured labourers (i.e. seven years of working like a slave with no money). Up north, the only people poorer than them were the Red Indians, so they mixed races. Then some of them took their families back to Scotland, to an island in the north. Now there are Gaelic-speaking people who are part big cross-armed Red Indians attending the Presbyterian churches in the freezing cold.

My aunt said I could come to Paris, to Ladders's studio, so long as I kept up my education. She called today and asked how it was going. I could honestly say, I'm trying.

God I'm dying for a pair of old-men's brogues, in my size.

Ladders and I had a long talk over my short past with men and his incredibly long past with women. I was going to cut my list down to three, but I didn't have a chance to do that because he got so uptight by number two we had to let it go. It seems that men always increase their conquests and women forget theirs.

We went to a Vietnamese restaurant and met this deliciously sweet actor who was able to put his belly on the table, and although he had all his teeth, they were the tiniest teeth I've ever seen in a man. He had a huge Roman nose. He'd been in trouble with the police over some prostitutes and I was riveted all evening.

NOVEMBER 22ND

Ladders has gone back to New York. I tripped over his meditation carpet and chipped my tooth.

Now I'm starting Alain-Fournier's *Le Grand Meaulnes*.

I'm sure this crisp weather is good for my skin.

It's amazing; I've stopped biting my nails and they are actually growing over the edge of my fingers for the first time in my life.

To get to the studio I have to cross through an apartment block. There is a grumpy concierge and a sweet cleaning lady who looks like Marilyn Monroe would if she hadn't taken the overdose and she'd boogied on for another thirty years.

I'm sitting in a café with photos all around it of the Quatre Arts Ball in the twenties: naked women painted completely in glitter with huge headdresses and pearl-buttoned shoes, men dressed as women, women dressed as men, students making human trains, baskets of white doves, miles of ribbons and fountains of champagne – blissful mayhem.

This was what I wanted when I came to Paris: decadence. Not all the time, but some of it. I had an idea about these wild brothels and the painters' models and guys like Modigliani and Toulouse-Lautrec drinking absinthe and singing in the streets. I wanted something wild but it really isn't the same, rows and rows of sex shops with litter curling up against their doors.

'There are more things forbidden to women than to men and so it is much more a challenge and a pleasure.'

I've been happy lately
Thinking about the good things to come . . .

1. wake up early
2. glass of cold water
3. not a lot of soup
4. exercise my mind somehow
5. fall in love
6. start on tangles
7. write letters
8. *paint* nails
9. no pillows
10. practice Spanish for the circus.

NOVEMBER 23RD

I can see through all of your lies
and still I miss you . . .

I must make the BEST of it all.
When, if ever, I get pregnant, I might shave my head.
This morning I met a foot fetishist. He is actually Sofia's boyfriend. I had heard about him before; he's a photographer she met back

in Rome. I had noticed how much time she spends either having pedicures or buying shoes. She spends a fortune on shoes and her apartment looks as though it was sublet to Imelda Marcos. She's had custom-made shelves built that encircle her doors to fit in all her pairs of sandals just, it turns out, to keep this guy. And do you know what? All those stilettoes and Gyorg (half-Scandinavian and half-French) has got half an eye on Sofia and the other half roving round every pretty foot on the block.

I was wearing a pair of forties stilettoes: oyster-grey with a red crystal button, hand-made in Italy and picked up for a few pounds at the Porta Portese market last year on a visit to my aunt.

On the night he left Paris, Ladders asked everyone at dinner if we looked good together. He seems to think about this a lot. I don't think about how we look, but I'm glad we went to Prague. If he comes back next weekend maybe he'll see for himself what I think I'll be telling him soon: The Lips.

'Hello, yes, it's Una, let me just get comfortable ... Of course I'm keeping the studio tidy ... No, I haven't binned any of your things ... I'm sorry to hear they didn't sign up Goulash after all your efforts ... It's true, Prague was special ... You know you're special ... I'm wearing my black painted kimono ... No, I wasn't playing with myself when you called. Actually I was working out my housekeeping ... No, really, I'm quite broke ... Yeah, I'm thinking about you too. There's someone at the door now, I've got to go.'

'Hello, yes, it's Una, let me just get comfortable ... I've missed you too, I couldn't concentrate on my studies today ... We can meet tomorrow ... I'm still thinking about it ... I don't know if I can wait till tomorrow, will you come and tuck me into bed? ... I know it's two o'clock in the morning and yes I do mean it. I'm wearing my white Victorian nightgown ... Of course I'm naked underneath ... Yes, I have. Oops, there's someone at the door, I've got to go.'

'Hello, yes, it's Una, let me just get comfortable ... What a surprise, how did you get my number? ... I'm really glad you like them, in fact they're my favourite pair ... Just sort of average, I guess, apart from where I broke my little toe, it went black for three days - Hello? Are you still there? ... No, I don't have a routine for them, I sometimes spray them ... Elderflower ... Well, it's a shame you just missed the summer ... No, I can't, I'd miss Sofia too much. Anyway, there's someone at the door, got to go.'

'Hello, it's Una, let me just get comfortable, I'm so hot, sticky - I'm wet ... Just a minute, that felt like your tongue was in my ear ... I'm going to put my tongue on you, across your chest, past your nipple and straight into the bush, my God, it's big, it's so big; I have to come up for air, aah ...'

I had to get a job and I didn't want to move from the studio. At the end of the alleyway there was a telephone box, falling leaves gusted against it, autumn leaves and hundreds of printed cards. They blew round my feet.

'Nineteen-year-old new to Paris and looking for a spanking . . .'
'Vietnamese flower will open for you, hotel visits. Call . . .'
'Dominatrix: cruelty, bondage, fully equipped dungeon . . .'
'Naughty Puerto Rican wants to play. Call . . .'
'Swedish erotica, no hurry, highly-educated, call this number . . .'

These cards drifted up to my door and got caught in the ivy. There were so many, they clogged my windows. I made a bonfire in Henri's mother's window box on top of her dead petunia and burnt them. One of the cards read, 'Telephone sex operator wanted, can work from home, call . . .'

I took the card back to the studio to show Sam and went to bed early.

The voice at the other end interviewed me.

'OK, chèrie, I'm a punter.'

I put on my deep and tarty voice and answered, 'Hello, yes, it's me, Una, it's just that my pants feel tight, can I take them off? I'll have to go to my bed . . . the lace on my knickers is cutting into my thighs. I'm going to peel my knickers off slowly; as I slide my finger over my hip, it slides down to my pussy. I'm wet, legs apart, thinking of you, there, standing over me. I love you watching me, I think I've been a naughty girl today. I didn't wear any pants when I went out today, you know, baby, you're the only one who can satisfy me. I

want to sit on your lap. Oh, oh no, I can't control myself, yeah . . .
YES, YES'

I heard grunts coming from down the phone, so it took me a
while to get that it was the interviewer trying to stop me to ask
a few questions.

'You have to get a mobile phone and we'll put it on the sex
switchboard. You're on trial for a week. All your calls will be
monitored. The trick is to keep the punters on the line as long
as possible as they are charged by the minute or fraction of a
minute.' I'd be on commission.

I worked like a dog, tidying the studio with a toothbrush in my
hair dressed in a dirty old tracksuit. I talked punters through the
mezzanine of a Neapolitan palazzo, in the Spanish Quarter, with
sunlight slatting through the shutters, waiting for my lover to
while the humid and sensual afternoon away.

My new boss rang after one of my calls and suggested I cut the
kimono crap and some of the architectural details. He said most of
the punters wouldn't know what I was rabbiting about. Do I rabbit?

I passed my test, my ratings were good. I had guys queueing up
on hold waiting for me to widdle over them down the line. Pissing
is popular and I have the weakest of bladders. I delve deeper
and deeper into my fantasies, egging on my clients, egged on
by cartloads of the most delicious foods delivered to my door.
I am locked into the studio by the food mountain outside
my door.

One day I get a very special client: it is Balzac. I talk to him for
hours and hours, kissing his toes long distance, sucking hairy feet,

I nibble the ankle bone, taking bits of foot to bed with me at night in case I get peckish, like the Andean rugby team with the fingers, like anyone in an aircrash in a landscape of shoes, like anyone with dreadlocks of telephone receivers all over their head.

There's someone at the door now - a crowd of McChicken sandwiches are knocking on my door, a queue of Burger Kings, a lot of ketchup.

Woke up to the phone ringing.

CHAPTER VI

From the moment I returned from Prague, The Lips had been coming on really strong. He asked me to marry him again (I think that is strong). I was happy as things were. He does a lot of things, he paints and he did something in films.

He looped me into his social life – it feels like he knows everyone here. My mother told me when I was a child and we travelled and everything seemed so big and strange, that actually it is a tiny little world at the top, like a pyramid upon whose tip everyone knows everyone. There are parties and dinners and balls, cafés, bistros and cinemas. The late-night movies are best, starting at midnight and then coming out to cruise in his beaten-up old Peugeot, shifting around the Café de Flore and du Dôme, out to his wonderful place in Fontainebleau, back to his flat in Paris, across to the studio.

He wanted us to spend every day together, to be together for ever and never leave each other's side. Well, he was telling me this and I thought, I'm going to try feeling this.

There were hours and even days when we were apart and every time I was away, I found it easy to get wrapped up in other things. He used to go off sometimes and spend till eight a.m. at a meeting and I'd hang out with my friends, mostly with Inès and Sam and sometimes Henri.

The Lips used to wear only black and I mean total, down to the Y-fronts. He was very intense.

Someone once told me that the way to test a lover is to travel with him. I tried it with Ladders and I have to say that he didn't bear up too well under pressure. With The Lips, I decided to test him at full force. First of all, we should go to somewhere noticeably lacking in the exotic. I stuck a pin in a map of England and it fell on Bristol. He was saying he wanted us to move to another country because I'd given him the strength to do that. So I thought, let's try the outskirts of Bristol and see how that goes.

We stayed in a little bed and breakfast and although he seemed a bit puzzled by the choice, he took it really well.

I thought he was god-like. I wanted everybody to see him. Women, and men, found him amazingly attractive – young and old they found him devastating.

It's quite hard to explain what he looks like because I spend most of the time focusing on his mouth, when he talks, when he's still.

My aunt came to see me. I met her at the Gare de Lyon off the night train from Rome. She had enough luggage for a decade in France. I was desperate for her to meet The Lips. We sat on the cold station concourse under an umbrella covered in pigeon shit while my aunt knocked back a double espresso and a brandy. Well, that was what she ordered, because no matter where we were, jungle, beach or mountainside, she ordered double espressos, making no concession to local custom or cuisine. So when her café filtre arrived, she grumbled and swilled it around the cup while I shared my new passion with her. I had loads of Polaroids of him on me, and I showed one to her. I'd told her about him and I asked her if he wasn't the most beautiful being she'd ever seen. She said, 'No, darling, he looks like a frog prince.' I didn't like her answer or her tone.

My reaction was to never, ever let her meet him. I hoped she'd come round eventually from worrying about what her future great-nieces and nephews might look like.

My aunt was big on genes.

I didn't care what she thought about The Lips's photo because I knew that, for once, she was wrong. I had photographs just and exclusively of his lips. He did have the biggest pair of lips.

Prostitutes don't kiss. I could be with these lips for the rest of my life. They are so intimate, the tongue behind them, showing when he speaks, when he laughs. We wear clothes to cover our nakedness, but our mouths are unveiled.

He keeps asking me to marry him; I don't know, how can I know anything when all I want to do is to climb inside his mouth, to kiss him and kiss him? I want to wrap his lips totally around me and inside his cheeks I want to find a little cubby-hole and move in and maybe after I've been there for a while I'll know, like people say you just know when it's right.

Did the Alliance française with my aunt. She buys me some winter clothes and completely stocks up my larder. She tries to interrogate me about Ladders's whereabouts, but I am too obsessed with The Lips to either answer properly or care. Before she arrived, I had borrowed a hundred francs from Sam to put some flowers and a bit of food in the studio to throw her off the scent.

While I escort her around the city, my fingers rub the image of my Polaroid.

Despite warning Henri and his clan to keep away while my aunt is here, he has sneaked into the shower while we were out. Rain drove us back only to find a large man naked in the studio.

Spent the evening staring into space. My aunt said I was 'just like my mother'. I don't want to have 'space to let' tattooed on my forehead, or all that fear.

My aunt has left for Spain. I have to return to Italy for Christmas.

How can I buy presents when this could be love?

How can I buy presents without any money?

For the next two weeks, I was playing Mrs Lips. The decision to get married or not was really out of my hands. I was too young. So my 'I will/I won't' are, technically, irrelevant, but they keep the two of us enthralled.

Ladders is in New York; he isn't calling me much any more. I heard a rumour that he is having an affair with a film star. I am less than gutted.

DECEMBER 20TH

Because I said I liked a song I heard on Van Morrison's *Astral Weeks*, The Lips has bought me a whole bunch of Van Morrison tapes. Van is now the man I spend most of my time with. He was seventeen when he was with Them and wrote 'Gloria'. He is the one person I actually go to bed with every night. I feel he will definitely be for better or for worse, for richer or for poorer, in sickness and in health until death us do part.

I heard that he used to eat a full English breakfast at a greasy spoon café in Notting Hill Gate in London. I dragged The Lips over there for a weekend and patrolled the pavement outside the café from dawn till lunchtime but didn't see Van the Man.

CHAPTER VII

Bit off one of my fake nails and had to take off the rest.

Eddie called from New York out of the blue. He asked how I was and I told him I'd met this guy whom I wanted him to meet. I invited him over. He said he would, but I knew he wouldn't. Eddie never argues and he never turns you down, he just doesn't do things. I asked him to come home for Christmas, and, of course, he said he would, but it's the same difference because it will be a cold day in hell when he comes anywhere near our house again. From a few months after Mother came home from her accident to the present day, Eddie pretends to himself that she's dead. Cinzia always says thank goodness she's just brain deadened enough not to realise how long it's been. Eddie was her favourite.

VIRGIN BRIDE

It is of huge interest to my friends that I am contemplating, even at the back of my mind, marrying as a virgin. Sam told me a story of a couple who'd been married for years and only after the lady had been to the doctor complaining of a sore belly button had anyone informed her that her kind of lovemaking was not standard procedure. Maybe it turned her on, but since she was also trying to get pregnant, who can say?

DECEMBER 23RD
The Lips took me to the airport. Suddenly now that I was going away I didn't want to let go of him. I cried all the way to Rome.

LE MARCHE, ITALY
The Lips has gone to the countryside for Christmas with his family. He invited me and I was torn.

I always loved Christmas, I used to be excited about it for months before, and I'd prise open all my presents and then rewrap them and put them back under the tree. My mother did a great Christmas. Now she's like a child but without the wonder. I miss her. When she's here with me, I miss her most.

I spend most of the time listening to The Lips's answerphone in Paris just to hear his voice.

December 24th
Dear Santa,
    Last year I sent you a list most of which just didn't materialise. I know you are very busy and maybe that list was just too long. This year, I have cut it down with a big effort; what do you say, we meet each other halfway?

    men's brogues
    bigger wrists

an amber cigar holder
an old Raleigh bicycle
a stocking stuffed full of milk chocolate
padded kimono – full length with blues in, maybe indigo?
Spinelli smoking jacket and cushion
a Japanese screen
a black opal – big
cowboy chaps
a notepad
scented notepaper (not lavender)
make my nails stronger than my will to bite them
black riding jacket
2 Persian cats
please add one cup size to my bra
and make Mamma better

CHAPTER VIII

I don't want to feel boxed in.

I'm not sure about this marriage thing and in six months' time I'll be old enough to marry and reality will kick in. I'll have to start being more careful.

I love the idea of being someone's mistress – mystery and passion and it all kept alive because of that edge.

My aunt's advice to me was always to keep a bit of a surprise in the background. After thirty years of being with my uncle, she said she still didn't really know him and that's what kept the relationship alive.

The Lips is a playboy. He has had so much sex. I think I was the first person he ever met who didn't want him sexually. After the initial shock, he seems to be really into celibacy with me. We have our kisses, and we sleep in the same bed, but apart from hugs, that is as far as it goes.

He says it's nice to wake up to clean sheets.

He has started leaving notes around the house, and before he goes to his studio, he leaves me a poem on my pillow. He lets me sleep in, which I always want to do now, so the day begins with lunch . . . one less meal to think about too.

Today he left me this:

Parisian male 21½
g.s.o.h.
seeks 16-year-old
half-Brazilian
for ever.

JANUARY 8TH

The Lips took me to an exhibition. Somebody had hired a detective
to follow the artist around and take photographs of her doing the most
mundane things like shopping or putting money in a parking meter.
She's called a conceptual artist. She also became a chambermaid and
when everyone had left their rooms, she photographed their rooms
and bathrooms, then had an exhibition. She is famous here in Paris.
I can't really see the art in it, but I think it's a very clever idea.

I haven't painted for over a month, but I want to start. I could never
do the chambermaid bit though, ever: 'Señor, your coffee is ready.'

Whipping out a little camera from inside my apron wouldn't really
do it for me either.

Eddie has written to say his girlfriend is pregnant and he is engaged.
This makes me an aunt. Eddie is nine years older than me. Everywhere I go, Eddie was there first; everything I do, Eddie has already
done. It's always been like that, with Eddie such a huge step ahead;
but I really thought I could take first place with a baby. I have always
wanted to have kids, while Eddie's interest in children is a negative

zilch. Now, with his own family, he'll be even further away from us. The news has depressed me.

Actually, maybe the baby will be an excuse for my getting near to him. I could babysit. Get some practice – but I'd probably need to get some practice in before I babysat. I shall ask The Lips to locate a baby here on La Rive Gauche.

I have moved so gradually from the studio to The Lips's place that I hadn't noticed until today that I have moved out of the one and into the other. When Ladders comes back, I'll have gone.

January 18th

The Lips had a dinner and his friends brought some coke. It was the first time I'd tried it. I've been curious for a while; I didn't let on that I wasn't familiar with the form. Out of courtesy, I was invited to go first. I was handed a hundred franc note which I knew from the movies had to be rolled into a straw. I did this and snorted. Nobody told me that the note didn't go right up my nostril. The coke glanced off my sinuses and shot to my brain. I grabbed my head before it fell off and staggered back to the closed window where I clutched at the pane until the coffees and liqueurs were finished. The Lips carried me to a chair.

Next morning, after a *very* long night, The Lips asked me why I hadn't said I didn't know how to snort, 'and nobody was wanting to use the note after it has been 'alfway up your 'ead.'

In this he showed he doesn't understand me at all. I will never admit I don't know how to do something.

✳   ✳   ✳

Like my grandmother, I'm a cheap drunk. One glass of Kir Royale and I'm a happy mess, two and I'm hysterical, three, I'm unconscious. Ladders loved this, it meant he didn't have to spend any money on my drinks when we went out and if he ordered a fabulous bottle of vintage wine, he could drink it all himself without appearing greedy.

Watched *Molti Sogni per le Strade* with Anna Magnani.

JANUARY 25TH

This diary could become like my first diary when I went to boarding school. It had a red leather case and a box with a key. No one was allowed to read it. It was totally secret. Inside, it read for week after week, day after day: 'Got up, had breakfast, lessons, lunch, lessons, supper, TV, brushed teeth, bed.'

The secret was, nothing happened.

It's a bit like that now, except no lessons. I've chucked in the Alliance française because The Lips and his friends are teaching me so much French.

I am reading Proust and sleeping a lot.

JANUARY 30TH

The Lips spent twenty minutes talking to another female at a party and completely ignored me. It was outside Paris in a château. I was so furious with him that I left with Inès and didn't tell him. I didn't feel like going out with Inès when we got back to Paris, and I didn't want her to stay. I went back to his flat and waited, working myself up into a jealous rage. I had the hot flush pacing fever and every drop of my Bahian blood was pitched for a fight.

I'd run through about thirty scenarios during my wait; I ditched the more dramatic ones and honed the forthcoming scene down to an ice-cold indictment of our shattered relationship. Our bubble of bliss had been pierced by some besaffaire tart who still wore a headband and turned her collars up.

The Lips came in, late and so pissed off from having searched the entire château and its grounds for me that it nearly threw me off track.

Within minutes we were screaming at each other and although his flat was quite small and cluttered, we managed to chase each other around it, locking ourselves in the bathroom and carrying on the row through the door. We goaded each other to unlock the door and come out, which we did. Sometimes, he'd pause and pour himself another glass of red wine, and I'd have a glass of Coke, then we'd resume the battle. It went on all night. I like this man.

January 31st

I am going to cook a meal for The Lips as a making-up treat. I have to find these ways; my older friends just take their men to bed.

The first time he came round to the studio and stayed all night, late in the evening he began to rummage around the kitchen looking hopeful and hungry. I didn't pick up any of his hints and the hours went by. His tummy was rumbling like Stromboli when he finally came up with 'What about some supper?'

I thought it best to put him straight from the start, so I looked vaguely around the room, sat myself firmly in my chair and said,

'Oh, I don't do food,' the way that some girls say, 'I don't cook.' Ever since, The Lips has catered for me, cooking all our meals and snacks. He likes to cook and we eat out a lot.

My point is so clearly made, I feel I could concede. I have a menu: it will not turn me into a domestic beast of burden and it will not include my old mainstay, the tomato ketchup sandwich. But it will include my only culinary speciality: the fresh fruit cocktail. Ever since I was a child I have been the mixer and sifter of fresh fruits and berries blended with wines and spirits, mint leaves, cucumber rinds and borage flowers for parties and dinners.

MY MENU
Parma ham and melon
4 lbs of best veal (sliced)
5 lbs potatoes (peeled and sliced)
2½ lbs of onions (peeled and sliced)
3 bay leaves – fresh
4 glasses of dry white wine
salt and freshly ground black pepper

PREPARATION
Cut all the fat off the meat. In an oven-proof dish, put a layer of onions, a layer of meat and a layer of potatoes. Repeat these layers until all the ingredients have run out. Cover with wine, plus two glasses of water, season and add bay leaves on top. Cover, sealing dish with a strip of flour and water paste to make it airtight. Put in oven at gas mark 4 for 2 hours.

SALAD: tomatoes – not too red and soft, salt, pepper, olive oil (virgin, cold pressed), fresh basil leaves

VEGETABLES: mangetout peas (2 lbs – do not *stew*)

FRUIT: grapes, pineapple, plums, pears

CHEESES: one mild – Bel Paese or Brie

2 medium – Double Gloucester, Cheddar, Taleggio, Camembert

1 strong – Gorgonzola or Stilton

Belgian chocolates, espresso coffee, real Turkish delight

wines – check this out with Sofia

2 types of water. Big jug of Bellini's (fresh peaches blended and strained through a muslin cloth. 1 part peach juice to 4 parts finest Asti Spumanti – dry)

white lilies, scented candles

TO DO

Suss out the wines and work out how much of the above I need for a dinner for two.

Through January, Ladders had left messages on the answer machine in the studio. Sometimes we'd talk. Well, we talked twice. It was clear that he had something going on in New York that didn't have anything to do with me. He was stringing me along, taking our arrangement for granted. I'd not been looking forward to any unpleasantness that might have come out of my thing with The Lips, particularly since it had so clearly overlapped with my staying at Ladders's studio. As luck would have it, I was the last thing on his mind that New Year. I told him I'd met The Lips, and he asked me if I found him attractive. I said, 'Devastatingly.' He did all this stuff about looks not being everything and older men being better lovers etc. Ladders is thirty-eight. He's rich and powerful and I don't think he thought for a minute I could give up the chance of being mistress to Mr Ludlow.

Am reading *Coming Through Slaughter* by Michael Ondaatje.

He came here and placed my past and future on this table like a road.

And:

'We'll go crazy without each other, you know.' The one lonely sentence, her voice against my hand as if to stop her saying it. We follow each other into the future, as if now, at the last moment, we try to memorize the face, a movement we will never want to forget. As if everything in the world is the history of ice.

FEBRUARY 6TH
The cold makes my lips stick out, but not like The Lips.

My voice isn't going to get any lower or sexier and I'm starting to smell. I'll have to give up Gitanes. Also my fingers are going yellow.

The Lips has brought me a video of *Terms of Endearment*.

The music right at the beginning has something about it. It's like telephone advertisements, or, in Italy, the Barilla Pasta ads –

they set me going every time. Right from the first moment when Shirley MacLaine pinches her baby daughter to make sure she's alive and then goes to sleep herself to the comforting cries of her screaming baby I found myself hooked.

Maybe it was because watching *Terms of Endearment* overlapped with the cold turkey off the Gitanes. The Lips brought me the film thinking I could snug up for an afternoon and forget my nicotine craving. It worked. I forgot everything. I watch the movie three times a day. I am exhausted from weeping. My eyes are so swollen and my nose so sniffed out and wiped, I need medication. Sometimes, after watching it, I just have to sleep.

The Lips returned after my first Nicholson/MacLaine session and he immediately assumed that someone in my family had died. He couldn't have been nicer. He comforted me for over an hour while I was unable to talk, racked by sobs. When he finally learned it was the film, he insisted on knowing why. What can I say? I am so spoiled for choice:

Obviously when Shirley MacLaine's daughter is dying of cancer and has put on some make-up quickly to say goodbye to her two young children.

And the bit where Shirley MacLaine has had to hold it all together, and she gets to the hospital cafeteria by the swimming pool and she sees Jack Nicholson there, just smiling, and she literally falls into his arms and you see her, held like that, sobbing and sobbing and she looks up at him and says, 'Who would have thought you'd have ended up being the nice guy?' Because Jack Nicholson is an ageing astronaut with only his past fame to pull the girls. They are neighbours, and they have an affair, but he disappears from her life when their love is threatened by the complications of her daughter and grandchildren.

Or when her daughter says she's pregnant.

Or when they're trying to get medication and Shirley MacLaine is screaming.

But really it's her character, all the way through, and her vulnerability under all the veneer of bitch.

I know it isn't Pasolini's *The Gospel according to St Matthew* or Bergman's *Wild Strawberries*, but this is the most emotionally cathartic film I've seen yet. It's like putting on woolly socks and a big cardigan when you get home at night. It's hot punch in winter.

CHAPTER IX

cut cuticles back to make nails grow quicker
definitely stop biting nails by end of Feb.
collect something – oriental children's footwear?
find out more about Brasil
read Jorge Amado
an old powder puff in a beautiful case
learn to cook
whiten teeth with bicarbonate of soda and lemon
buy a half veil with one of those little hats/headband
find fragolino

Have started going for walks. I take the concierge's dog out because she's old and doesn't have the time. It is a beige cocker spaniel – Edouard.

I miss my studio, if only for painting. Now I've left the Alliance and I have nowhere to paint, I feel myself drifting. I hope The Lips finds me a space soon.

FEBRUARY 10TH
Only eight weeks to my birthday. I'll be seventeen. What am I doing?

FEBRUARY 14TH

Felt-tipped kisses all over my naked body and waited for The Lips with a white rose and a vodka with fresh raspberry juice cocktail, fizzed with champagne. He arrived late with a card; the drink had gone flat and scummy and the ink on my body had smudged off.

CHAPTER X

Had a discussion with Inès about sleep. She thinks I'm a freak of nature because I can sleep anytime and anywhere. At school I had a knack of seeming to be awake while I was actually sleeping. I sleep with one eye open, like a snake.

I am one of those people who has to sleep a lot. My mother always used to tell me that you can only grow in your sleep, and I'm still growing. But also, your body's cell proteins can only renew themselves when you are asleep. So, in fact, rather than being a social leper, everyone should really imitate me and sink comatose at the dinner table a couple of times a week.

Since I moved out of the studio I have been having the longest dreams. Sometimes, they are so long that I just have to wake up and get out of them because I'm exhausted.

The Lips has located a studio for me on the rue Vavin – it's perfect – it's a bit of a long way to go, but I'm so sluggish at the moment, I think the fresh air and the exercise will do me good, especially on my bicycle.

I'd like to foster a child. I mentioned this to The Lips in passing over dinner. To try to please me he said he thought it was a fabulous idea, but his friends tell me he went apeshit.

I'm not sure about the mangetout peas for my dinner party menu – maybe broccoli is better, in lemon or wine or something.

I want to get a granny's shopping trolley with a wood frame and a cloth bag – you know, like you see under the stairs of double-decker buses.

I want to meet somebody who does something interesting in their life and really enjoys it, and, say, who only comes to Europe to refill his camera bags and to get a new commission for a book. Someone who is mysterious and a bit of a recluse and an adventurer – uncluttered by too many possessions and complications, not stuck in a social brothel somewhere.

When I was a kid, a photographer turned up out of the blue to see a friend of his who'd been staying with us. His friend had gone back to London, but my mother asked him in anyway and he stayed a while. He arrived in an open-top black bashed-up car and there was something about him so intriguing that when he left, my mother and I both jumped into his car. All crammed in (it was a two-seater, or maybe the back seat was full of junk), we rode to the outskirts of town, to a junction where the motorway began. I didn't want to get out or let him go – this stranger. I was eight years old and inconsolable. Then he left and I never saw him again. His name was Livingstone. No first or surname, just Livingstone. My aunt says she heard he'd ended up in a desert. He had wild black curly hair and black eyes and a tan. He obviously didn't care about his clothes and he was just right.

To this day, an open-top battered black car has the smell of safety to me.

God he was nice! Since then I've named many teddy bears, and my dog in Italy after him, but, frankly, it's not the same.

I need:
   a piece of fresh beetroot (it tends to go slimy, so it has to be fresh
      and I must remember to throw the old bits away more. After
      slimy, they shrivel up like little black rocks. The Lips thought
      it was hashish and tried burning a bit)
   Vaseline for shiny eyelids
   blusher and fat brush for permanent warm glow
   cover concealer for when the Jeanne Moreau look isn't wanted
   small mirror in my make-up bag at all times, disguised to look
      like something else. If anyone moves, loses or touches it, I get
      very upset.

Went for a walk in the Bois de Boulogne and found a little skull.
I'm going to start collecting skulls.
   Also met Kiki there sitting on a bench.

Coffee with Kiki: she knows a lot about Man Ray and Cartier-Bresson and Frida Kahlo and Angelica Kauffman and Georgia O'Keeffe.
   Out with Kiki again. The Lips was livid when I got in late.
   Lunch with Kiki and The Lips is OK about it because she came and picked me up. He was relieved to see it wasn't a man. Big mistake!
   I'd never been chatted up by a woman before. Kiki looks incredibly feminine, but when she gets to the point of asking me out, it is in a very masculine way. I can see why men find her very attractive.

She keeps singing something under her breath:

This could be the perfect fit.
. . . They can't understand the magic . . .

Separate from my diary, I keep a manual for my mother. The diary
is for me, the manual is for her. It's mostly pictures of me and my life
during all these years that have passed her by. One day, if she wakes
up, then she might wonder what went on in the years when she was
out of it. I was ten when it happened and I'm nearly seventeen now.
A lot of things have changed. I've changed.

In Prague I caught a lot of greys for her – at least eighty shades:
a blind man in a grey street shuffling over the cobbles; me and
Ladders on the bridge – we got another tourist to take the picture
like the tourists do on the Ponte Vecchio. And I take photos of my
mouth, of my hands and feet. I know mothers are into all that.
We went on a school trip to the Isle of Wight, there's a museum
there with plaster casts of babies' hands and feet like a forensic lab,
like a careless morgue, whatever, but it turns out Queen Victoria
had all these moulds made of her kids' hands and feet. She had
nine children. Maybe the moulds were to stop her from muddling
them up.

A lot of the old people in our village are dying. Every time I go
back there's either a funeral or I've just missed a funeral. I want her
to remember these people whom she wanted me to grow up around.
That's why she moved to Italy.

Now I've got my own Polaroid I'm filling up my manual much quicker. Even if I just lie in bed, I photograph the room for her, the bed, and when I seem to be doing nothing, I feel like I've got a purpose.

The whole manual thing makes Eddie cross. He says it's sick. He thinks I should just accept that our mother is never coming back any closer than she is now. He likes my being in Paris. I came here for myself, I wasn't running away from anything, but he can't see it like that.

I photograph the empty streets of Paris from the roof terrace at night, bits of the embankment with the clochards sleeping underneath the bridges, the Luxembourg Gardens and the rue Fourbourg Saint Denis that never sleeps. It's comforting.

A friend of The Lips says he would gladly eat at the Pompidou Centre every day because it's the only place in Paris where he doesn't have to look at the Eiffel Tower.

I used to borrow other people's Polaroid cameras to fill up my manuals; or when I was younger, they'd be snapshots and cinema tickets and my entrance to the ice rink. And I'd put glue on the paper and wipe sand across from all the places I've been to without her. I do the manual more out of habit now, or rather I did, until I came to Paris and here it seems more like a way of reviewing my life myself. I want to make some sense of it too. And I realise that I don't just write my diary for myself, a lot of that's for her as well, so she'll know me like I know myself.

And it's drawings, little sketches of benches where I first met people, the signs of cafés where I took a first coffee.

I won't fade away unless I want to . . .

Kiki has given me a sheep's skull she found by her country cottage. The Lips says he won't give it house room unless I soak it in bleach. I think that's a bit anal. I bleach it and lots of little brown maggoty things float up to the surface of the bucket. They are disgusting.

Kiki is beautiful, but I don't think, Cor, I'd like a bit of that! She has a really seductive laugh and she has a way of walking with you with her hand round the back of your neck. She's got a lot of red velvet slippers. She always wears very big cashmere wraps. I highly approve of her dress sense. She takes me shopping to the flea market and insists on buying me things. Doing the flea markets together, I suddenly find I have someone to spend my day with. It's too claustrophobic to be with The Lips day and night, I have to get out, I can't be caged in.

We go to art galleries in the afternoons, and to her flat for tea; Earl Grey and chocolate fudge cake – this woman understands me! She says she understands me more than any man could. That she holds the keys to all my problems.

We talk a lot.

She tells me I'm destined to be with a woman and I say 'Hold up – I haven't been with a man yet,' that's first on the to-do list. When she sees me and The Lips together, she observes our relationship with such disdain that I am going to keep them apart from now on.

Kiki tried to kiss me, and I was curious. She said tomorrow I am to go to her flat and lie on her bed and she will show me things. I can hardly sleep wondering about this.

On the way back, I let myself into Ladders's studio and listened to his messages. The tape was full. Something happened a few days ago, as though he suddenly realised his bird has flown. He says he's coming over.

All the way round to avenue Victor Hugo I kept asking myself why I was going to Kiki's at all. On arrival, we started haggling over her seduction. She has an enormous fur rug on her bed and panels from theatre sets around it. She has vases of immensely tall white lilies. For three days she'd been sending them to me and it was really starting to freak The Lips out.

We lay in bed and she stroked my hair and held me. I didn't think once about the situation as it was happening, she made me feel good. The night before, I'd imagined Kiki in a black leather mask, whip in hand, chasing me around her flat with a large wooden dildo strapped to her stomach.

At school we had gone over every aspect of sex, but it had always been intended to be with a man.

That evening, as I wandered back along the avenue Victor Hugo, my brain was racing.

CHAPTER XI

I dreamt that Kiki took me to London.

She takes me to a huge studio full of sculpted heads and fragments of bodies all made out of white marble or cast in bronze. A lot of the heads are bandaged like stuff by Mitoraj. All the rest is bare and the wooden floor is white like ash. In the centre there is a big fur rug. Kiki comes up through the fur rug from the floor and the next thing she is on top of me, forcing me. She puts bandages around my face and then tries to put me in a cast. She is going through a list of her favourite sculptors of the last fifty years. Then she says, 'I can't let you waste your life on men, this isn't going to hurt, my sweet angel, just go with it.'

A cement mixer appears. It begins to pour cement over me. I become a pillar, the cement has nearly reached my mouth. I cannot move. I am screaming.

Next morning I get a note.

Una, darling,
    If you ever change your mind, you know where to find me.

Meanwhile, please don't let my studio go to waste.

    yours,

      Kiki

On one end of the fur rug there is a pillowcase of cash. I get tired of counting before I've finished adding it up, but there is over two thousand pounds. That's a lot of food.

The studio is down a little cul de sac, between a betting shop and a workman's café.

Once you get in to the studio, it is absolutely fabulous, but the mews itself is a notorious dumping ground in King's Cross. It is ankle-deep in sodden rubbish; at one end, a sofa plays home to a drunk, at the other, little piles of discarded needles mount up the damp brick wall. Gutters are broken, doors battered, and what look like a series of garages are actually the rooms of a group of prostitutes. So the place is not only a favourite open toilet for the neighbourhood but also a well-tramped knocking shop.

I don't know what to do with myself here. I don't have any books or friends and all of the city seems to be closed every time I go out, except for the fast-food chains. I try venturing out at different times to catch the city awake, but it is not possible. So I ferry take-outs to my new flat and watch the cardboard boxes getting trampled into the alleyway as tramps rifle through my rubbish bin and chuck everything on to the road.

My only contact is with a pimp (who seems delighted to have young fresh blood on his doorstep and is constantly trying to enrol me), and also with his girls. As the weeks go by, the girls and I bond silently.

There are six of these girls, then one of them leaves and there are only five.

One day the pimp disappears and all the girls come round to my place for a make-over and to use the phone. I offer to make their calls for them. I book their punters. I am very organised. I write down the names and details of all their clients in my diary. I take Polaroids of them all and stick them in my manual.

I give them all a serious make-over and completely restyle them. The improvement is spectacular. Limousines begin to queue up all the way to St Pancras station. The girls blossom.

I pretend that I like the girls all the same, but I have a favourite, Pearl.

Sometimes we spend pleasant afternoons just lazing around with Pearl looking at all my clothes, trying on my kimonos. Pearl has good music which she brings round, and an endless supply of hot pepper sauce. She's about twenty-four and has a great face and body. She has hair extensions. She's a good businesswoman, she teaches me how to manage our funds, she takes no shit from anyone. She wants to stash as much money away as possible and thinks she has a vocation for this job. The men say she is a miracle. She is fully booked. I buy her presents, she tells me details about her punters that make me laugh. She tells me I'm uptight and I should screw some of the customers. 'It would help out in the rush hours, and it'd do you good, girl.'

We start a cooperative; the money piles in. There is a soda fountain at the bend of the stair and a fruit stall outside my bathroom door.

Every time I go by for a wee, the cockney stall-keeper calls out, 'Bananas, only a pound a pound — dead useful in your line of business' or 'Pomegranates, two for fifty p. The symbol of fertility, very sexy, must go today.'

Two of the girls don't get on with each other, they come round a lot and complain. Some of the punters complain about them too, but bit by bit they improve and I keep scrubbing them down and working on their look. Mara is Algerian, she is only a year older than me. Her face could look interestingly exotic with a lot more work. The problem is her body: it's designed so that all her food (and she likes her food) falls down and cradles round her ankles. I give her one of my old kimonos and insist that she wear it in her bedroom up until she is literally on the bed doing it. She also has a huge ass, but that can be an asset in this business.

The garages are torn down and replaced by sweet new rooms, colour coded for the girls. Pearl's is oyster and opal; Mara's is red and gold; Jezebelle, youngish, Colombian, with a pretty face and a body that looks like it had been swapped at birth with someone else's and a very loud, grating voice (which I am working on), has blue. Vanya, our Polish intellectual with black hair and blue eyes and who is beautiful with a boyish figure, goes for sage green. Emily, who is English and a bit plain but scrubs down nicely and can look great with her make-up right, has pink.

I end up spending a lot of time with the girls. I get to know their secrets. I love dressing them up. It's like dressing dolls. I put Jezebelle into simple gypsy-style clothes, small loop earrings and nineteenth-century shawls. She doesn't get that many customers, they tend not to rebook her, so she and Mara are more at a loose end. Jezebelle is actually quite bright even though she started out on the streets of Medellín and her expectations weren't high. Just getting to London had seemed like hitting the jackpot and she hadn't done anything else to get a better life other than spread her legs from the day she lumbered down the stairway at Gatwick airport.

I become the Madama of the Mews. I learn a lot. Jezebelle and Mara start to blossom, but never lose a certain flow of jealousy and spitefulness towards the other girls.

I persuade Pearl, the Jamaican, to throw out her hair extensions (which is weird because I always wanted hair extensions myself) and to cut her hair to an inch all over. She's a real corker. She has the most beautiful skin. She's also chronically lazy — which I can really relate to, and addicted to the Ricki Lake show and anything else going that bares souls live. She zaps endlessly through the satellite channels. The only times we fall out are if anyone interrupts her while she is watching one of these shows. She will perform all the usual sexual acts as advertised in telephone booths and magazines, but she wants these shows blaring reassuringly beside her. Most of the punters just put up with it. If anyone really complains, I back Pearl up, give them their money back and let them go. If I had to screw a queue of sleazebags, I'd want to have Shirley MacLaine beside me on the screen, or Anna Magnani.

Having said that, some of the punters are drop dead gorgeous.

Some are hunks, some are short, tall, fat, greasy, spotty, noisy, sweet.

I am most interested to see how they are really just like everyone else. Not any special type.

My girls get so popular, the traffic jams and queues go beyond the railway stations one way, and beyond Coram Fields in the other. The police come and make a fuss. The two officers come into the mews. They begin undressing, folding their uniforms up very neatly into piles. The mews is clean now and full of Russian vines. The policemen put their truncheons one on top of each pile and walk naked across the cobblestones. One has a very long thin willy like a dog, the other has tight balls like king marbles and a tight ass. One goes to Pearl, the other to Emily. Pearl's one says, `I insist you switch off that chat show in the name of the Law.'

Pearl says, `Fuck me, baby.'

The television says, `Larry has been two-timing his wife, he doesn't know that is why he has been called here today, come in, Larry.'

Deafening applause. Whistles and stomping. Clapping so loud, I wake up.

CHAPTER XII

Ladders arrived at the studio and I wasn't there. He began looking for me, with Henri, Inès, Sofia and Sam and all and any of my other friends and acquaintances. They didn't give him my address, but they called and told me. Also that he had found one of my lists with a note on it talking about how attractive I found this guy and us playing happy families. Since I had never said I found Ladders attractive, later he told me how much this hurt him.

Kiki has gone away somewhere.

He called home to Italy and he looked for me all over Paris until he discovered that I sometimes ate breakfast or went for coffees at a little café near Pasteur.

Because I was a bit drained by late nights with Kiki and because I had a cold, I didn't go there for a couple of days. But Ladders took a table by the window and sat there for three days, stacking up coffees and wearing down his nerves. When the café shut, at midnight, he stayed outside it, sleeping on the pavement in the rain and the cold.

Friends of mine did go to the café on those days and they told me he was there. He sent notes to me via them. The first one was brash and confident: 'Yes, he's young and I'm glad you've done this, but how about being with a real man?'

By day two, he was more appealing. By the evening, he seemed desperate.

I had never seen Ladders vulnerable. I suppose I didn't really care for him the way he was usually, quilted with power, taking everything for granted, assuming it was always a greater pleasure for me to be around him. When he got desperate, though, and he didn't know where to turn and he just slumped against the café door in the rain, I felt very drawn to him. He'd thrown up his pride to the wind. He wanted me so much he didn't care who laughed at him. This was a side to him that he had done everything to mask. It explained a lot of things about him and his lists suddenly made more sense:

I must achieve
I must be strong
I must achieve
strength is power
power is protection
I must never break the circle
I must achieve
if I achieve people will like me

The next note came out from the crumbling façade: 'I know what's wrong. I view my life as though it has ended, as though I'm summing up all the achievements that I have made. But I haven't achieved anything and that drives me to distraction. I live my own obituary, and one day I'll find my life has ended – and I haven't enjoyed one moment of it. I know I should live from day to day and moment to moment because that's what's supposed to count. You are the only person who could help me to live like that. I've started to imagine that I'm dying as I fall asleep again.'

This guy is seriously fucked up. Maybe he could be my greatest achievement.

So what if he's not a genius, he's got a real talent for picking what's good. Some of his bands have been going for years.

The Lips was disgusted at the way Ladders was trying to hunt me down. He said it was all emotional blackmail to get me as a possession, a trophy. Lips had never really taken Ladders seriously.

Meanwhile, another note arrived, this time brought by Inès with a little packet.

Darling Una,

I bought this ridiculous pink ring in California for you. I haven't had the chance to give it to you, so I'm asking Inès. And here we are – and what a tangle.

Una, just be a doll and let me know what's going on. I won't bite. I love you too much. Whatever it is – whether you needed to be on your own for a while, or whether you've fallen for someone else or whatever – please write or meet me and tell me. Do me at least this honour.

And if you want me, I'm here.

I love you.

Ladders

P.S. I go to Brasil on Tuesday – want to come?'

February 22nd

I went over to the studio to meet him. He looked a complete mess, unshaven, dirty, desperate – much more my kind of thing. Then he got down on his hands and knees and asked me to marry him. I said, 'OK'.

The Lips was upset at the idea of this sixteen-year-old girl going off to look after this much older man. He was sure I'd just go on holiday and come back to him. But Ladders had touched me, he'd said the right thing at the right time. I went back to The Lips's place to tell him I was engaged to Ladders and had to collect my stuff. He watched me pack in stunned silence. I didn't have an explanation.

CHAPTER XIII

Flew to London with Ladders. He wants to fly over to Italy and rent a car and go to Le Marche to ask my mother for my hand in marriage. It took the entire flight and the ride in from Heathrow to dissuade him. He had planned this little concert, him and me, with my mother at the centre, taking the news graciously, ecstatically (I don't know what the hell he imagined. Had my mother been able to take it in, she would have been horrified), and Cinzia, popping the fragolino to celebrate. He didn't want to take on board that my mother's brain damage could extend even to matters that affected him. Eventually, he realised how it would have had to be, with my mother in her wide-brimmed hat trimmed with the tattered strip of Thai silk rotting round the rim, and her flat basket on her arm, wandering round the garden, with Ladders and me trailing along behind her, talking into the winter wind.

Our garden is a beautiful place. All the house is covered in climbing plants: wisteria, jasmine, clematis and roses. They ramble, but the garden is quite organised in its way: it has lots of flagged paths that divide off different sections. My mother planned it when she was younger, when she was well. It was the same design we had had in other gardens, identical, so we all knew the twists and turns of the paths as though by instinct. My mother is an obsessive weeder. She was fairly excessive about path-weeding before the bus, but since the accident, she spends most of her days pulling out stray blades of grass or creeping clover. Cinzia says the maze of our garden is like a brain and that Mother keeps the one she can clear because her own is so irrevocably clogged. All I know is that my mother is constantly stepping from one section to the next and that the only way to talk to her is to follow her around and address her disappearing back. No matter how much you keep up with her, it is always as though we can never get into the same part of the garden as her.

It's the same for anyone who comes. Sometimes a hopeful art student turns up from her past and it's just the same. Questions are only ever answered by her bland 'Lovely, darling', regardless of what they are. It is her answer to life, a blanket approval, a devastating indifference: 'Lovely, darling' as a response to birth, death, joy, pain, and all the bits in between that life can come up with.

I'm going to Brasil and I don't even have a bikini, let alone a thong.

Ladders has invited my aunt to a meeting. We're leaving for Rio tomorrow evening. Ladders offered to fly via Rome, but my aunt said she welcomed the chance of a trip to London and she's coming over for tea this afternoon (as one does).

It was all supposed to happen at Claridges and be quite formal and Ladders promised to say nothing to my aunt about the situation.

Ladders broke the news, joking to my aunt in the back of our hired Mercedes on the way back from the airport. First she looked at me, and then very slowly at him, and then more slowly she said, 'Hmm, that's wonderful', in the most unrealistic way, as though I'd just shat on her head. She didn't believe it, thinking it was another of my passing fantasies.

The one thing my family had really drummed into my head like a mantra was not to get married young. I was supposed to get an education, to go to art school, to do something with my life, to be something. But I thought, Huh, I want a bit of what they had. They'd married young and I didn't for a moment go for all their stories about how it was different for women then. A woman's a woman, and I wasn't thinking, except to believe it would be the whole package and this was the first piece of the jigsaw.

And I thought it was all right that Ladders was over twice my age; because my father had been an 'older man', I liked the fact that Ladders was. If I'd met him when he was young, I don't think I'd have paid him any attention. I thought he would be able to see any pitfalls ahead and I'd be safe with him in Brasil.

And I liked what he did, that people came up to him and recognised him. The fact that he wasn't as successful as the people he hung around with was only galling to him.

Over the phone, before she came from Rome, my aunt had warned me 'not to do anything stupid'. When we got out of the car, she motioned me into the ladies at Claridges and sat me down in one of the little boudoirs with its extended dressing table and its vase of white freesias and a pile of laundered face towels. I could see us both in the mirror – we looked good together. I have her nose.

She had one last try, much to the delight of the lavatory attendant behind us who I could see was tuned into radio drama live.

'I'm totally convinced if you marry this man it will ruin your life . . . and make wretched your destiny.'

This brought the biggest lump to my throat.

'You are so special, Una, but you're not special enough to overcome a bad marriage.'

I cried like a baby, so long and loud that my aunt said no more and merely closed me in her arms. Over her shoulder, in the mirror, I saw there wasn't a dry eye in the house.

There had been a little bit of me wavering. I hadn't slept the night before, worrying, but my aunt made my way clear. She is one of the most original people I know and she has a knack of saying just what I need. There, in the Claridges' loo, by some curious chance, she had warned me with lines lifted word for word from *Terms of Endearment*:

> The world has gone mad today
> And what's bad today
> And black's white today . . .

Ladders kept saying how he would be ready to marry after Brasil and how he wanted a wedding that would make up for all the years that he'd never got married. He envisioned it in Le Marche, at my mother's place. He saw it as a huge Italian affair. I thought: Whatever, and started practising my Portuguese.

Ladders kept saying, 'I want it done now so you don't change the way you feel.' I took this for passion.

When the idea of Brasil came up, I thought suddenly: That's so far away, and I wanted it. And it was South America and I was South American. I was excited just by saying the word. All my life all I'd ever heard was 'God, you must be Brazilian' because of my mix. But Brasil is so big on a map and it's vague. People didn't say, 'You must be Bahian.' I expect, like me, they didn't really know where Bahia was. I seemed to fit other people's image of Ipanema beach. So I felt I'd be going somewhere I belonged.

Before she died, my grandmother got a travel bug and hot-footed it round the globe. She made a trip to New Zealand and Tahiti, and another to Greece, and when I was eight, she went for two months to Mexico. Since this coincided with my summer holidays, she took me along for company. My memories are few. Mexico City was red and dirty and we both got diarrhoea. Guadalajara sold hamburgers, Mendoza didn't. But I do remember my grandmother telling me as we stood in the big square in Mexico City that she had brought me there to find my roots. I was eight years old. The people there had straight black hair and different looks altogether.

I'd done some looking for my physical roots: checked out lots of bits there in Central America to find a place where I'd fit in and look like everyone else. I didn't fit in in Europe, but going to Brasil would be it. I was going home.

Just the words, the words I'd been waiting for, the password, like my father's: 'South America.'

And I thought I would be safe.

CHAPTER XIV

RIO DE JANEIRO, FEBRUARY 25TH

We are staying right by Copacabana. As the plane was landing, it was set to crash straight into a mountain; everyone crossed themselves, including the air hostesses. I can't stand turbulence so I was already imagining my funeral – me looking absolutely radiant in the coffin and a lot of people who weren't invited being able to kiss me.

Five guys from the Italian football team are staying at the hotel and they've all had their passports stolen, so there is some mass hysteria.

FEBRUARY 26TH

Ladders is off doing some record deal.

The manager of the Italians tried to pick me up yesterday by the pool. I hung out with him again today. He took me round Rio. I'm getting used to this – hanging out with other people. I don't know if this is the way it's supposed to be.

As we go round the city, the manager gives me lessons on which are and which are not child-bearing hips. It is the year of the World Cup and he's going to see if he can get me tickets for the key matches.

* * *

Ladders is busy in a recording session somewhere. He gets off work really late – I hardly see him.

One of his runners has got some tickets to *The Leopard Show*. We queued up to get into this sort of theatre hall. There were no posters outside, nothing about the show, but it was packed and everyone was dressed really smartly. We were sweating like pigs. It was thirty-seven degrees C.

The auditorium was very steep, the lights went down, and when they came up, there were fifteen men in shiny trousers and little vests. There was a huge round of applause and their trousers seemed to slide off, leaving them in thongs. They had the biggest dicks I'd ever seen, even in my dreams. King Dong would have been among his brothers. Apparently they'd been picked from all over Brasil. They all wore leopardskin things – hence *The Leopard Show*.

The lights went down again, then the thongs came off and there they were with their penises limp. An usherette came round with all these roses and flowers and the audience threw roses at whoever they thought had the biggest dick.

The guys went backstage, and reappeared fully erect. One of them had this big gob of sperm at the end of his dick and it dropped on the stage and he nearly slipped over on it. The man with the most amount of flowers by his feet got a crown on his head and he had to pick someone from the audience to dance with on stage.

You have to remember that they are not only completely naked, but there are bits of sperm dropping off their willies. So they danced for a bit, then the lights go down and it's finished.

FEBRUARY 28TH

It is really getting to me – I don't have child-bearing hips. All these shapely women are giving me a complex. Even the men have great hips.

I'm eating chicken and rice – excellent, and gumbo – not as good as my mother's used to be.

Flak from Ladders about the state of our room – my clothes.

look into hip transplant/padding
coconut water
learn the lambada
find superglue for nails
work on Ladders to adopt street child – children?
write postcards to Inès, Sofia, Aunt
sort out laundry
buy thong to take home; I'm not ready to wear one yet because I
    look like a boy from behind. Everyone here wears thongs and
    they look great. Apparently if you have a lot of children you get
    big hips. Live in hope.

When you think of Rio you can't help thinking carnival, and since the Carnival was on while we were there, as soon as Ladders got an afternoon off, we went up into the stands and had drinks and squished ice and watched a sea of dancers surging past. It was so massive, biblical, and hard to imagine so many people together all locked into pleasure. I felt religious fervour or something like that, like seeing light. Then Ladders said it was absolutely amazing because he'd got some tickets actually to join in.

MARCH 1ST

We were watching *the* biggest crowd and the schools of dancers when he said, 'I've got a surprise for you.' He took me down to one of the samba schools and we were to dance in the Carnival itself, me in a bikini with the biggest fucking headdress and a ball and chain round my leg – and it wasn't a non-heavy one. I was then chained to another person – a woman built like a brick shithouse with saddlebags implanted in her hips. She was not impressed with my footwork. I felt if she could have cut me off at the ankle, she would have. Ladders had a ball and chain too, and boxer shorts and a video camera. The camera was quickly confiscated by one of the slave-drivers who whipped the dancers on and kept the school in order.

Ladders and I looked at each other in horror as we were separated and driven on by these scary meatballs. As he yanked me through the crowd to join our school, he told me proudly that we had paid seven hundred dollars *each* for this humiliating and terrifying experience. In the mêlée, Ladders's power didn't seem to exude in its usual way. He told me later he'd tried to bribe someone to unshackle him, to no avail.

Meanwhile, as the meatballs kept whacking us, I struggled to learn the intricate samba steps of our school. This was not a wiggle your hips to the music with a slug of rum in one hand and a smile on your lips. It was deadly serious and the most concentrated thing I'd done for a long time.

Half an hour in, I was dancing like a queen from the knee down;

but my head was dragged back by the tube of metre-high feathers wired into my hair. The end of my plumes was two people back behind me. There were literally millions of people around me, and above me were walls of cheering spectators banked either side.

The thug kept pushing and shoving me. I could hardly move, and I kept trying to pick up my ball so I could manoeuvre better, but it was shackled short to my leg, and it was really heavy. Which was all bad enough until my headdress got locked with somebody else's headdress like fighting deers' antlers. I not only caused a whole chunk of our school to slow down (a disgrace beyond description) but I nearly got my head severed at the neck and for a moment I felt a whiff of lynching.

'Miss Otis regrets she's unable to lunch today, madame.'

March 3rd

Maybe it's the way I dress, and I am not referring to the incident at the Carnival, but I'm still being looked at in Brasil as though I were different. I thought I would just melt into the crowd, but I don't.

It is fantastic just to be in the sun and to be able to eat lychees and mangoes. As to the staring, I guess I'll have to get used to it as I am with someone nearly old enough to be my grandfather.

When Ladders's recording sessions were finished, we flew south and rented a car and went to a kind of hotel compound with little cabins. It was directly on the beach. The sea was not quite as crystal clear as I'd expected.

For once, I wasn't projecting somebody else, I was Una, a girl going back to her childhood in South America, tasting the tropical fruits.

MARCH 6TH

Ladders wants a scuba-diving card to slice in with his credit cards. We are in a tiny thatched cabin on a concrete platform on a white sandy beach.

I played hide the laundry with him. As he showered, I managed to relocate my two bags of washing from under the bed to outside the back window. I knew he was about to start his ritual tidy-up. I hadn't even got up the aisle yet, and he was already distressed by my slobby habits. Little does he know that he ain't seen nothing. Out of respect, I've been keeping certain things away from him for months.

My aunt had lectured me before I left for Paris about clothes on the floor; picking them up, washing them, and putting them away. I failed on two out of three of these counts. At home I failed on all of them. My pathetic excuse was that I was born to a different station in life and I grew up followed by maids whose job it was to pick up the trails of debris I left behind me. My aunt tried hard to be a reality check.

I told her, 'Yeah. I know I was only five when all that stopped; but I can't help the four hundred years of inbreeding behind me – cousin to cousin. My God, can't they see it's a miracle I can actually get out of bed sometimes and walk about a bit?'

Well, no, Ladders can't see that miracle and he takes a dim view of my dirty laundry, antique dresses, lace shawls etc. They are, in this tropical heat, heaving. It is forty degrees centigrade in the shade.

Soon, I won't have to move them around, they'll get up and walk by themselves. Until then, I have to keep up my mission and hide them out of the window as best I can while dorm inspection takes place.

I have to send a card to Inès and a letter to Alessandro, the first person I felt dizzy for.

People say that a first love is special, that it means we have something special between us, we were each other's first love. I am glad about this because he's one of the nicest men I've ever met and probably will ever meet. It's like a little locket we wear round our necks.

The manager of the hotel has hair that looks like a toupee – I think it is, but the maître d. says it is a transplant from his body hair. Whatever, it's a big mistake. Every time the manager speaks to any of his guests, he thrusts his head forward so his scalp is right under their nose, so they can't miss it. He is obviously really proud of it, and if he's happy, I guess it's OK.

I've worked my tan to a native Indian shade – glowing red-bronze. I tried aloe vera straight from the plant as recommended by an escort girl at the hotel in Rio who took a shine to me, saw I was bored out of my mind and put a few tips my way – she had skin like silk. She also mentioned that if marriage didn't work out, I could make a fortune as an escort girl in Rio. She gave me her card.

Head to toe in transparent aloe vera slime, lay on beach for hours, coated in sand – I wasn't even approached by the coconut-sellers.

MARCH 7TH

We went down to the sea, to the bay for the first day of the scuba-diving course. The water is so clear and warm it's like stepping into a bath with tiny coloured fishes swimming around your feet. It smells like a freshly conditioned head of hair. We turned up at exactly seven a.m. and met our instructor – who was about my age and looked much younger.

We waited around in the heat for other people to turn up with our scuba gear, then, finally, we convinced him to take us out on the boat. Ladders was stifling in a size too small wetsuit. The instructor gave us a thirty-page instruction manual from the seventies in Italian. Ladders complained, but all that was left was Italian. I couldn't get my rubber gloves off, so Ladders was turning the pages while I translated. We'd got to page seven when the boat stopped. Those seven pages of warnings had been enough to convince me that I didn't want to go. After all, it was Ladders who wanted the scuba-diving card in his wallet. I didn't even have a wallet, let alone any credit cards.

When the moment came, he was over the side like a boy scout at a Jamboree, which left me trying to take my mask off because I didn't want to go in, prior to some serious sunbathing on deck. The instructor didn't believe me. Underneath all the rubber I was too hot to move. Exhausted by my abortive efforts to remove my mask, I paused, slumped on the side. My temporary limpness was taken as a sign of consent and the instructor bundled me over the side of the boat.

I was spooked. I'd been spooked even before I hit the water, it was just one of those days when I jump at my own shadow.

The next thing I knew, I was going down fast. My tank was firmly attached to my back, Ladders was nowhere to be seen, the instructor was nowhere either and I was at the bottom of the ocean, alone.

I could hear my breathing all around me. I had my eyes closed. I remember touching the sea floor, then I began to rise and I don't remember anything else. It felt like a blackout, then, gradually, sensations began to come back. It was dark and it was cold. The one bit of comfort was a warmth between my legs – I'd peed myself. I was just starting to adjust when a surge of grey matter tried to swallow me up. The one thing I'd remembered from the guide book was the word 'shark'. The one thing I'd remembered from the manual was the emergency cord on my suit.

. . . in caso d'emergenza, pull cord to go up.

If we'd got to page eight, I'd have seen that you never go straight up without stopping and timing your way to the surface.

Although I couldn't see him, the instructor was there and helped me up. The grey thing came up with me. It would not let go. I couldn't breathe. It was all over my face. When I got into the boat, it changed colour. It was going green.

I was lying on the deck. My instructor was trying to rip it from my face. It wouldn't let go – a huge octopus – it was going to eat my face and I couldn't scream as it was already down my throat. Bravely the instructor battled with this creature. He said something in Portuguese like, 'It'll be OK.' Then it came off, and he fell back, and I knew it wouldn't be OK because he was gagging, and Ladders's voice was near me in the boat, 'Jesus Christ, that is disgusting!'

There was a bit of dialogue over me about the degree of grossness. When I finally opened my eyes, I was confronted by two shocked faces and a maskful of snot.

CHAPTER XV

According to Molière, 'Everything in the loved one is lovable.' Yet, already, I don't love his meanness and he detests my squalor.

I dreamt I was on a yacht with a foot fetishist.

It is just the two of us and he's someone I know, but he won't take his shades off, so I can't recognise him. He looks a little bit like River Phoenix and a little bit like my dad. He has a big hamper with all the fittings and china and silver flasks like the one I want. He unpacks a picnic in a field. It is all laid out on a Turkish kilim. I eat, but he doesn't. He says, 'At picnics, your feet are on the table, do you know how delicious that is?'

My feet are on the cloth. He tells me, 'Ever since I was a little boy, my only real sexual pleasure came from feet. The rest is going through the motions.'

I don't care. I love him.

His job is to photograph models' feet as they step out of taxis all over London. I go with him sometimes. None of the models really like him; when his back is turned, they grumble about the disproportionate foot maintenance.

One day, stepping out of a taxi, I have a miscarriage. It is a little girl with gold earrings and curly hair. When he sees the baby, he says, `You never told me about Copacabana,' and he dumps me.

Much later, by mistake, I get an invitation to the opening of his exhibition about the taxi feet. I toy with the idea of turning up in the most fabulous pair of shoes he has ever seen. I toy with the idea of breaking into the costume museum at the V & A and stealing them for the evening. And I toy with the idea of turning up in Birkenstock sandals (which he sometimes has nightmares about). In the end, I don't go. In the end, something else happens, but I can't remember what.

Collected bits of coral and some shells.

put lemon juice in hair
swim
eat more fruit
skimmed yoghurt
find somewhere that does gumbo
sketch

Today packed my bra with loo paper and instantly made my breasts two bra sizes bigger – a miracle! To think that I have been asking Santa to do this for me every year since I was twelve. It seemed like a lot to ask at the time and somehow more forgivable that he couldn't rise to it. Now I see that all that was required was a bog roll, I feel outraged at the mean old bastard. I cannot wait to get back to Paris to parade down the Champs Élysées with my new knockers. Just once. Meanwhile, I have taken them to the hotel bar for a Coca-Cola.

Every evening, Ladders likes me to dress up for dinner. I go along with the dressing-up thing, like I did with the 'Señor, your coffee is ready' and I suppose I will to other things so long as they don't get really over the top. Inès told me that a friend of hers gets money from a guy for inserting fake nails up his bum while he tucks into a tub of of popcorn. No way, hosē.

I have made friends with an old guy on the beach. We meet up after breakfast and hang out, or after lunch if that isn't possible. He is eighty-three. We talk a lot and he's got lots of funny stories. And he can push out his false teeth to emphasise his point.

Beware of men whose eyebrows meet,
Because in his heart there lies deceit.

Not so in Alfredo's case – he has enough facial hair to qualify as the wolf man, and it's all silvery.

Alfredo says the only thing that mars my beauty is that I don't brush my hair at the back.

Jack Nicholson invites Shirley MacLaine to dinner; she turns him down. Two years later, on her fiftieth birthday, she rings his doorbell and says she'd like to go to that dinner after all. He points out it was two years ago; she says a date is a date, and that is the beginning of their romance.

If a date is a date, does that mean I can go back with Alessandro, my first love, and put right all the things that I did wrong? And are The Lips, and all my friends in Italy, are they still there for me, with their lives on PAUSE while I live on?

And for Alfredo, heading towards seventy years of loves and lovers, does it mean they are all there, all his? I don't think so. It must be more like picking up bits of shell and keeping them as a souvenir of much much bigger things.

In the evenings, tree frogs the size of Smarties make endless noise.

MARCH 10TH

DRINKS

    coconut water

    fruit cocktails: maracujá, guava, mango, papaya, etc.

    sparkling wine

    fragolino

    milky drinks

    juices

    Evian

    eliminate Coca-Cola

SNACKS

    nuts and raisins

    dried fruit

    fresh fruit

    healthy sandwiches

eliminate chocolate, sweets, cakes, biscuits and crisps

Saw *The Cotton Club* in Portuguese. I think those usherettes' trays
with the straps are so sexy.

I've been sketching a bit. I got one likeness of Alfredo; my aunt
says if you scribble around enough one of your lines will have to
fall into the right place. I don't know if I'm any good as an artist,
I want to be, but I just don't know. We'll be going home soon. I
don't know where home is going to be, Ladders is a bit mysterious
about it. One thing's for sure, though, wherever it is, I'll be ready.

put on 3½ kilos of weight on hips and tits
exercise to build up and tone up and get muscle to firm up
3 big meals per day
snack as much as possible, always eating
max. 3 cigarettes a day – don't inhale
finish latest manual and send back to Italy
do preparation for doll
mend and dye clothes and shoes
to think of Ladders as more eccentric than barking
find Robert Johnson tapes

Long talk with Ladders about Memphis.
Spent the afternoon walking through grounds with Alfredo. He is
leaving tonight. The trees and shrubs are so huge and healthy here,
I want to dig them up and send them back to my mother. Reading
my last list, am appalled to see all the things missing, like:

singing lessons

guitar lessons

British passport

styling for mags, videos and films

manual driving licence in London

get automatic car

get a dog – Neapolitan mastiff?

find some charity work

thread veins done (don't know exactly what they are, but have
them done anyway)

teeth bleached and hole treated

get small tattoo

get grey Persian kitten

go and see Eddie and not let him go

I want to be in love. I want a soul mate, I don't want it dull, there has to be passion.

If I take away the staring, and the fact that I can't understand dipshit of what is said to me, this is home. Actually, there has been a big improvement in the last week, whole sentences are sifting through. The intenseness of the heat and the darkness of skin, an undertow of sensual music are all in my blood. I grew up hearing about people whose eyes are too close together and who fucked donkeys, and who were basically living an upper-class *Deliverance*, squealing like pigs on the fantastic plantation that had been in my father's family for so many generations. As a little kid, there were lots of people in those coffee groves who looked very much like me because we all had the same grandfather.

I used to feel it was nice to have that romantic notion: 'I am an heiress.' I realise now, 'heiress to what?' To a wide patch of baked mud and some seriously shrivelled-up coffee bushes – Borbon Salvadoreno: that's the coffee my father grew. After he died, it seems the estate died with him – ran to weed, got subdivided into little strips of beans and squash.

Since my mother lost it, I have had some serious weed training – an intensive weed-pulling course. But I hate weeds in a different way than she does. I refuse to have anything to do with them. If I have to take over my inheritance, I'll be dragged into that jungle bound and screaming. It's all a dream anyway, because before I get press-ganged into responsibility, there's Eddie. Primogeniture, the firstborn, the male. Goddammit, the upside of such a male chauvinist country is at least that my brother must be first in line for martyrdom on the family land front.

MARCH 12TH
Chicken and rice, chicken and rice – I love it.

Ladders is doing some research into the duration of the siesta and the depth of sleep.

Someone left *Tin Tin's Destination Moon* on the beach. It is mine, ha ha. I read it in the bathroom.

Met an Italian woman, she is a fashion editor in Rome, sort of knows my aunt. Gaia says she is an artist, she has perfected the art of grafting, she has successfully grafted pure pleasure on to her job.

I lay beside her on the beach and she told me lots of gossip about people I'd never heard of and about clothes. Gaia is on full expenses here, she has been shopping in Rio, her luggage is a golf buggy job, she has eleven Louis Vuitton cases and boxes – her magazine will pay the excess. She makes me laugh. I can see she likes me (no Kiki stuff here); she invites me to Rome. I tell her I might be getting married. When I say it, I start crying.

Once, when my mother was getting back to the earth, we lived up a dirt track in East Anglia. She rented a sixteenth-century collapsing cottage with no bathroom and an outside loo. She used to tip buckets of blue stuff down the loo which was in a little shed at the end of the garden. She used to think it was fun; Eddie and I thought it was the end of the world. Once a week, a big muffled lorry used to creep up to our cottage at night. Men in a kind of black combat gear, with masks over their heads and faces with only slits for their eyes, nose and mouth, used to leap out of this lorry and crawl around our garden. They'd run from apple tree to apple tree, up to the chemical toilet, then retrieve the inner bucket, carry it back to their lorry full of shit and crawl back to replace the empty bit. They were called, collectively, The Night Soil. Everyone in East Anglia outside the towns knew who the night soil were. But we didn't come from there, we came from Salvador de Bahia. We weren't used to masked men hiding in the flower beds at two o'clock in the morning. The first time we saw them, we nearly caca'd ourselves. Later, with time, we got a little bit more used to them, but the strangest aspect of the night soil was that all the men were anonymous. It was such a nasty job, and all the men had, of course, to be local, but no one ever wanted to admit to working for the night soil – hence the masks, and even more sinisterly, their total silence. They never spoke. If you said good evening or good morning, they completely ignored you. Anything, whatever you said, they pretended you weren't there, they never replied. All you'd see in your flashlight would be the black woollen masks and a pair of glazed eyes staring through you.

As the tears welled in my eyes at the beach bar with Gaia, she stirred her caipirinha and stared through me in that same way. It was a total 'I cannot see you, you do not know me, I do not know you, this is not happening'.

As soon as I got my emotions back under control, she was there for me again, full attention as we discussed hemlines and watched scarlet macaws circling over the beach.

CHAPTER XVI

There's a photograph of me, aged four, on a tractor. My mother told me I'd been allowed to drive it on the fazenda. Ever since, I've had a thing about driving. I learned to drive in East Anglia when I was twelve: at that point, we had a huge garden and I used to drive round it.

In Italy, some of my friends let me drive their cars. In Paris, I'm such a cheap drunk, I tend to pass out, so I don't really drink, which means I get to be chauffeur to friends coming back from nights out. As long as it's a motorway or a fairly straight road (strictly no parking), I can do it. So I'd had quite a bit of experience and it annoyed the hell out of me that I couldn't get a licence because of my age. I thought it was a complete injustice against me. Ladders never let me drive – I suppose because he once saw me abandon a car in Pigalle.

By the beach in Brasil, at the end of our stay, as he was having a long siesta, the urge to drive got the better of me and I took our rented car for a spin round the outskirts of the hotel compound.

It was March 12th, I'd spent the morning on the beach with my friend Gaia and then had the beach buffet lunch with Ladders: a hundred exotic dishes served in tropical splendour. I had the rice and chicken.

Driving that car was complete enjoyment: me cruising along admiring the scenery, the radio playing Gaetano Veloso; coconut groves and sugar cane.

I rarely check my back mirror, so I didn't see them coming, they were just there beside me in a flash: two policemen.

Something was said to me in Portuguese which I didn't understand. I said I was English. One of them asked where the car papers were and my passport. I told them, 'Back at the hotel,' which I don't think they understood very well.

I've stopped, and the younger of the two is asking me questions. He is very polite. I gather I am to go with them to the police station and everything will be fine. I have to follow them in my car, which I do.

By this point I am thinking, 'Oh my God!' I am in such shit because I'll have to wake Ladders and he'll have to come to the station for me, like some naughty schoolgirl.

Then, when we got to the back of the police station, to a car park or something a bit beyond the building, we stopped. I wasn't really thinking except, What am I going to say to Ladders?

The younger policeman got out of his car and came to talk to me along the lines of: 'Do you like my uniform?' and 'Do you like my gun?' He pulled the gun out to show me. I wondered what the hell was going on. His colleague was looking uneasy and wandered away.

My car door was open, the young cop with the gun in his hand was standing by it, and then he whipped out his willy.

My first reaction was disgust. He had this vile little thing out. Then I suddenly realised what was going on and I thought, Oh no, here we go! It hadn't occurred to me until then because they were policemen. When you need help, you call the police, so there was no one to call.

I did what he wanted and thought of England, Brasil, Italy . . . He'd pushed the seat back. I had these dungarees on, and one of the buttons had come off and I'd done it up with a safety pin. He couldn't get it undone and it made him very angry. He kept kneeing me. He tried to do all this penetration, but it just wasn't working. That's when he got really aggressive.

I remember thinking of a list while it happened, as in: if I survive this, the things I am going to do.

At one point I looked up and saw the older one. He was just looking at me. He had his dick out too, waiting.

The young one talked to me all the time, saying things and slapping me around. What did he want me to say? 'Oh my God, you're fantastic'? The one on top of me kept licking my face. Like lick, as in LICK, which was really obscene.

I kept hearing cars going by, not very many, but a few. Having this guy on top of me, I was in a position from which I couldn't actually move. And, by the way, we are talking halitosis, and licking my face; I thought I was going to barf.

✳   ✳   ✳

It went on and on.

One of the main points was he was impotent. He couldn't get it in and he was so aggressive. He was shoving other things in me. All the way through, I had the gun right there at my head. He put it in my mouth, in my ear. Ladders's lighter had fallen out of my pocket, his special one, initialled, and I wasn't supposed to have it, and that got put inside me too.

At the end of it, the young guy said, 'That was good, you were a good girl.'

They got me into their car and drove off. I thought, This is it, I'm going to be killed and dumped, and this is Brasil, there'll be a piranha fish lake.

We drove past the scuba-diving shop and the guy who'd taught us to scuba dive the week before was there, outside. I was crying and banging on the car window because I thought I was going to be killed.

I had been a long time.

Meanwhile, Ladders had woken up and looked for me, found the car missing and got upset. He was outside the hotel when we drove up.

He said to me, 'Now you're really in big shit, you're under age!'

I was hoping that he'd know what happened. I was caked in sperm and I'd been beaten up, there was blood on my face.

I said, 'These people have hurt me, they've hurt me.'

He kept saying I was under age. 'Go inside, you're in a lot of trouble.'

He was so angry with me. I looked back and he was paying the policemen, giving them money so there wouldn't be any hassle about the car. He drove off with them, and I didn't feel safe any more.

I tried to scrub myself really hard. I just felt that he'd let me down. Not them, him. Then I went for the aspirins and by the time he got back I was still in the shower and quite far gone.

I didn't let him in. I didn't want him to, didn't want him to see me. But he got in and saw I was really beaten up. He cried and apologised for not having seen before.

I said, 'Fuck you.' It felt as though he had just paid them to have sex with me. I felt dizzy and sick.

The next thing I remember was being in hospital and having gallons of stuff forced down my throat and being pumped out. They said it was just in time but my stomach was perforated.

All I wanted was to go home to Italy, but Ladders said no. 'We have to do this properly, to get them and get justice.' I thought, What about me? It had happened to me and I'd survived it, but I was numb and I felt incredibly ill. I was in pain and I wanted to be able to go back home instead of watching Ladders go through a complete crisis about the fact that he hadn't noticed. So it became about him and about dealing with justice, despite there never having been a Brazilian policeman charged with a sex crime before. Ladders kept telling me how important this was for me to deal with; but I didn't care about any of that stuff.

I actually didn't want to talk about it at all with him. He wanted to go over and over the details. I said, 'Why torment yourself? It's done now.' I didn't want to talk anymore.

It shattered my idea of men in uniforms because he was really a vile creature, that policeman.

A week later, we left. I didn't want to be with Ladders. I didn't want to see him or touch him. So I came home to Italy. He'd let me down.

I remember feeling old, really old. My face was still battered and the immigration people at Fiumicino Airport didn't let me in because I didn't look like my photograph. I didn't fit my age. They refused to believe I was sixteen.

My aunt came through and got me from the detention room where they held all the illegal immigrants, and she took me home. I don't even remember her pulling me away from Ladders at the airport.

CHAPTER XVII

I just wanted to come home to my family. I wanted my mother, and if I couldn't have her, then I wanted to be near her shell. I wanted to smell her and to touch her freckly hands.

Le Marche, June 25th

Aretha Franklin is downstairs somewhere singing
'A woman's only human . . .'
   She stops singing and someone else takes over.

   Voices and songs drift up from the kitchen.
I've lost myself. Just in this last week, I've started looking, sifting, sorting. I've always loved beaches, lying on them, walking along them, looking out over them, dreaming about them. And I like to pick up stones and shells. I'm picking myself up now.

*   *   *

To get here, you drive over the mountains on a windy road and then you come into a valley and there's nothing there but countryside and the lake. There are wild boar in the woods and they come out sometimes when you're peeing on a walk. They crash through the bushes and charge towards you before doubling back and running away. After a long bumpy track you get to the house, and there's that feeling that there is here and nothing else. You can drop your bags by the door and just wander around, eat when you want, you know, really relax.

The whole place is rambling – it's falling down like a Neapolitan palazzo without the hustle and bustle all around it. There are piles of discarded terracotta and mounds of stone moulding waiting to be put up or sorted out. It's been there so long it's like an architectural feature. The house is incredibly big, but it doesn't actually have many rooms for its size. Each room is enormous and there isn't a lot of furniture. We spend a lot of time outside on the terraces.

People have come to stay and do things in the house: plaster, pave, dig, build steps in the garden, or whatever. They've all left their mark on our house.

As we drove up this time, it was the same old singing echo from the back of the house. Dante is an opera singer who's been living in the back flat for years. He knows all the arias from Puccini and Verdi and he whacks them out day and night. He's very hairy and intense. He has a huge appetite and makes up buckets of pasta with chilli and garlic and eats like a horse. The muse hits Dante all over the property. If it weren't for the muse, I think he'd be a famous opera singer, but as it is, he's constantly writing poetry.

He has the same appetite for women as he does for food and life. He is voracious. He pursues girls through cobwebby corridors around the house. He roams the streets of the surrounding towns looking for girls. Sometimes, when he's really broke, he makes his money by busking, or rather singing in the street. His voice is so wonderful, people flock to him. It's the kind of voice that makes windows and glasses practically crack, and some women's nipples lift to the sky.

He's like that big spider who stuns her mate and carries him into her web. His southern hormones exude, and despite the tufts of hair that struggle up through his shirt front, Dante gets laid regularly.

Sometimes he brings girls back to our house. He once turned up with some Russian dancers who'd been studying eastern dancing – candles on your arms and feet. He emptied out the fridge and then shagged these girls all night with such gusto that the whole palazzo echoed to the thudding of his iron bedstead on the plasterwork.

Il mio mistero è chiuso in me . . .

I love that aria.

I just wanted to go home. I didn't want to have to explain everything or anything. I wanted the bruises to fade and for the attack to just be a memory.

On the train from Rome, my aunt and I came up with the story of a car accident. We knew there'd still have to be a lot of questions because Italians are incredibly nosy and want all the details of a disaster. If I'd told them what had actually happened, I would have had to keep going over and over the details, and they would all have been so shocked and upset. They couldn't have changed anything, made anything different, and the whole village might have sunk into post-traumatic stress.

We hadn't bargained for the obsessive national interest in cars. The reconstruction of my accident was exhausting and I kept getting it wrong on cross-examination. Within days, I decided to stay in, and then, gradually, to stay upstairs on the second floor in the immediate vicinity of my room.

When we first moved here, I was scared of being alone in the house. It was derelict then and had no doors or windows. I went for the smallest room in the middle of the second floor so I'd be wedged in between everybody else. They all had to come past me to get up and down the stairs or to go to the bathroom.

Because it was square, it was like walking into a big cupboard. It has a mattress on the floor – to Cinzia's horror. After camping for six months in the derelict house, everyone else got fabulous antique beds from Venice, hand painted or hand carved, but I kept my mattress on the floor and 'chose to live in squalor'. I had pictures leaning up against the walls: portraits by my mother of family and friends and three framed sketches of me.

When we arrived, the plaster was cracked and beautiful fading pinks and creams, stained and aged by damp and sunlight. That was how I wanted to keep it so I varnished it over in loads of different layers – anything from two to ten, to get even deeper variations in the shades of pink.

In the middle of the one outside wall, the medium-sized window is always kept shuttered. I like the darkness that comes in broken from filtering out the sun. It's a lazy heat that creeps through. In summer, people in the village tiptoe around their houses trying not to wake up the heat inside them – the shutters are closed, the lights are off, doors are shut and blinds drawn. Then in the evening, you wake up the house and the world starts up – air circulates, smells are released and movements are pulled out of their slow motion.

When I went into my room on Wednesday, the bruise was nearly black, purpling around the edges, a little bit darker than Ribena before you add any water. By Saturday, there was a hint of raspberry. Then there was a blue and a yellow with green thrown in. It was shaped like France if you took away the Normandy coast. It started above my left knee and disappeared into my knickers. It was darkest on my inner thigh, but even that mark faded, and I was left with no visible trace of that policeman. The bruise on my right cheek, which travelled across to my ear and down to my throat, stayed yellow the longest. It stayed yellow for months. It was the last stamp to go.

Who would have thought you'd have ended up being the nice guy.

I moved the video recorder into my cave and watched *Terms of Endearment*.

* * *

When I got back, my mother was in the herb garden. She was weeding the brick paths. Sometimes, friends of hers worry what she will do when she runs out of paths to weed. The herb garden is the answer to this question, it is a vegetable version of Brooklyn Bridge. Without the use of chemicals, no one could ever keep the herb garden fully weeded, not singlehandedly, anyway. The maze of brick paths is a seed bed for every weed in the neighbourhood. My mother spends a lot of her time there. Cinzia has helped her to plant sage hedges.

Cinzia believes in the healing power of sage on the head. The longer my mother stays there, the more she inhales.

One of the most amazing things about Cinzia is not just that she has stayed with our family for twenty-six years, devoted to my mother's caprice, but that she actually seems to enjoy it. She sees mess as a challenge and cleanliness a victory. She goes around after my mother (and me when I am at home) dismantling the accumulating mess, mopping up the mud trails of Mother's gardening boots. Cinzia also tracks down the desiccating heaps of excrement from the stray cats my mother collects.

I shuffled past the low sage hedges towards my mother and held her in a tight embrace and accepted the half-hearted pat she gave my shoulder gratefully. This was her stock response. I looked long and hard into her eyes and she looked back long and hard into mine. Her eyes flickered their usual bland smile with a glimmer that I had seen so many times before, a puzzled look of 'Do I know you?'

If you need some affection,
My arms are open

JULY 3RD

Woke up and watched *Jules et Jim* and ate crostini with minced ham and mayonnaise constantly.

I realised for the first time today how hard Cinzia must be working in the kitchen.

Cinzia is healing me with food. She ferries trays up to my room with all my old favourites. They seemed to appear as though by magic, dreamt-of but unasked-for takeaways. Now I see she has a policy: she is wooing me away from my depression with recipes from our shared past:

penne al pomodoro
crostini
Milanese escalopes
zucchini flowers with cheese
wild boar rolls
lasagne
spit-roasted chicken
cinnamon toast
salami
cheese bread
tiramisu
trifle
mascarpone cheese beaten with egg yolks and sugar

spaghetti with smoked salmon
Irish stew
feijoada
gumbo

And zabaglione, that backbone of every Italian childhood. Put two egg yolks in a cup, beat them with a fork until they whiten, add two spoonfuls of sugar and beat again until the mixture becomes almost transparent, waxy, add a drop of very strong, cold coffee, stir and eat.

'Mamma, I'm tired' = 'Eat zabaglione'.
'Mamma, I'm sick' = 'Eat zabaglione'.
'Mamma, I'm dying' = 'Eat zabaglione'.

A cup of zabaglione a day keeps the doctor away. Five cups a day makes you very, very constipated and, over a period of sluggish months, turns you from a slim person into a woman of rounded curves.

JULY 18TH
Watched so far:

Belle de Jour
Vive sa Vie
Caro Michele, in which Mariangela Melato plays 'a hippie full of courage and aggression'

Nanà

I Vinti – like all those jokes: there was an Englishman, a French-
man and an Italian . . .

Un Borghese Piccolo Piccolo, with Alberto Sordi – my favourite
Italian actor

Eva, with Jeanne Moreau

La Provinciale, with Gina Lollobrigida – La Lollo

Borsalino – Jean Paul Belmondo, your lips!

Terms of Endearment – of course

Molti Sogni per le Strade – Anna Magnani is a goddess

JULY 20TH

I am in a cocoon, safe, fed and transforming. I am going from thin
to fat, from weak to strong, from young to old. I have given up clothes
except for sweaty 1940s slips.

AUGUST 8TH

If . . . If . . . If things had been different, Ladders would have been
trying to marry me today.

My aunt came up from Rome to see if I was OK about it: the
anniversary of a rocket that never took off. We talked about Ladders
– well, she did. She asked if I missed him. I told her I'd come back to
Italy to be with my family, I didn't want to see anyone else. Ladders
hadn't had much choice in my decision to come home, but he'd
kept calling.

Cinzia and my aunt hadn't the heart to tell him to what degree his
fiancée was changing, not only physically, but towards him. I refused

to speak to him. Even when a phone was brought to my room. I was changing into something that he was no part of. I was growing into my fantasy world, giving it new horizons, leaving behind a lot of luggage. He was a part of that luggage. I'm changing carriages while Ladders is full speed ahead on his menopause express: toot toot!

It was as though I was in a soap opera and he was behind the camera directing my every move. I was on show and on set so much of our time together. Now the star of the show was taking over the picture, and in pure Hollywoodian style, I was letting him go without so much as a goodbye.

I'd left it to my aunt to tell him, which she did, over the phone. He'd been wanting to come out since April, but I wouldn't let him. It wasn't until the end of May that I felt able to tell my aunt quite what Ladders's part in the whole affair had been. She was outraged.

Next morning she left for Rome, disgusted, angry and disillusioned with Ladders; wanting to see him locked up, strung up, castrated and run out of town.

Cinzia tells the rest of the story. Ladders arrived next day. He wouldn't take no for an answer, he wouldn't leave.

For four hours he hammered at my bedroom door, alternately whispering and shouting sweet nothings through the keyhole. Cinzia brought him occasional refreshments as he pleaded on the landing.

He kept telling me that no matter what it took, or how long, he would always be there for me. That this was true love: 'We were made for each other, whatever role you choose to play now will always be the one for me.'

By early evening he was hoarse and had taken a chair. Cinzia had joined him, knowing that what was there on the other side of the door could, in some ways, alter his professions of undying love. Ladders went to a lot of trouble to be cool, this much was clear to Cinzia, and nine-tenths of my attraction had been my skinny and fashionably exotic looks. In that process from cocoon to butterfly, I had reached the larva stage. I was fat and sallow.

He kept going because he was powerful and used to having his own way, and because he was stubborn, and guilty, and because he could see us in his mind's eye at some fabulous party for some golden album produced by him. He'd be getting slapped on the back and having his rectum licked out and I'd be the envy of all his friends. Lastly, but probably not least, he'd invested a lot of time and several air tickets in our romance and he didn't want to lose that cash.

Eventually, sick of having the video soundtrack full blast to drown his entreaties, I turned the key and let him in.

It was dark and it took some time for his eyes to adjust to the surroundings. He had cried a lot that afternoon, and his breath was short. I couldn't say if it was me or the sudden rush of airless food vapours that made him gasp. When he finally saw me like a beached whale on the bed, he flopped and landed beside me. If you're not used to sleeping on the floor, it's always a lot further down than you've bargained for when you do that. He lunged out and hugged me. The armful was obviously a lot more than he'd expected, and I felt him tense. His mouth searched mine and clamped down over my lips. The combination of my favourite garlic chips and the slight growth of hair over my lip was more than he could deal with. This was a session not even he could manage. It had been our first and our last kiss.

He mumbled something about time and space and backed out of my room. I heard him commiserating in a hushed voice with Cinzia outside my door.

It was clear he wasn't going to spend the night and the next thing I heard was his hired car speeding across the gravel to the gate and tearing down the dust road.

CHAPTER XVIII

AUGUST 15TH
Movies and food, food and movies.

AUGUST 17TH
If ever there was a me ME ME MOMENT, then it's now, and I need to be in it, and I also need to get out of it. I feel I'm dancing with a ball and chain.

I am almost tempted to open up the shutters a crack and read a couple of books.

My aunt keeps offering to get me professional help. I don't want that, I want time: to heal, to lay some memories to rest and to come to terms with not being a child any more. I am no longer a little girl. Eddie knows this. He didn't come running this time. He wrote. He's waiting to become a dad. He's busy. I know it isn't that he doesn't care, it's more, here is something Eddie wouldn't want to admit happened, let alone discuss.

Once, my grandmother accidentally slammed my finger in our car door. I saw my finger dangling from my hand and it wasn't something my mind favoured to rest on. Already, the memory had faded. Now

I needed to fade this newer thing. Time was pushing it back. I just need to keep fading it, chasing it away with other images, enough to drown it. I'm getting there. Sometimes it feels less real than *Roma, Città aperta*, and sometimes I can laugh again.

I laughed when my aunt went over Ladders's flight. And I laughed the day I woke up, three weeks ago, and my middle didn't ache. And I laughed when I saw a news clip of 'the top men of the pop world get their rocks off together'. It was a huge party full of rock stars all seated round separate tables for six. From the placement at these tables it seemed there had been some serious wife-swapping. But the jiggery pokery was confirmed when the hands of the rich and famous went surreptitiously into their heads as they scratched at the head lice they didn't know were there.

Way back, before Christmas, Henri gave me a headful of lice. I gave them to Ladders who took them to London and New York before having a number two crew cut himself. Ladders had given them to a singer he produced, who gave them to her real boyfriend, who happened also to be seeing someone else who had a one-night stand with the Russian girl who's bonking the lead singer from . . .

I saw their indiscretions mapped out so plainly and televised, and I imagined them going half mad with the tease and crawl of wandering head lice.

When the videos stopped, the screen would flick on to a classic movie channel. I saw only black and white movies, I didn't deal in colours.

I want to reread *If This is a Man*.

AUGUST 20TH

I am becoming a chemical sleeper.

Every time I cross the landing to use the bathroom, I am wearing a pair of stilettoes and my slip. It is as if I am living in a boarding house somewhere in Rome in the late forties, locked in a script, waiting for something to pass. I selected twelve films and rotated them.

Cinzia kept hinting that maybe there was a good film on the other channel. She would sweetly sit and watch some of the films with me, but would be asleep in minutes, twitching the muscle under her right eye, upset by my piles of discarded clothes and the general state of dirty mugs, crusts, crumbs and apple cores on my floor.

AUGUST 22ND

Woke up to Dante whacking out *Tosca*.

I can't decide whether to get up or not: the family curse has got me. For months, I haven't wanted to get up – so there's been no problem. I crawl out of bed to switch videos and haul myself across the landing to wash or pee. Now I want to get up, I can't make up my mind. This is something inherited from my father's side. From him I also get:

my dress sense
obsessions – from inbreeding, I presume
pathological laziness with occasional spurts of frantic energy
phobia of injections. No heroin/junkie sermons here: it took six
   nurses to hold me down for an anti-tetanus jab
bite nails

From my mother I get:

> the dark rings under my eyes
> big eyes
> big hands
> a desire to paint
> a love of travel
> a sense of accomplishment from little things
> my fantasy world

AUGUST 24TH

Woke, still groggy from a dream, and looked up and saw myself in the mirror. My hair had achieved the perfect look all by itself. Magnani's hair looked as though she had just got out of bed from her lover, tousled and full of split ends. I had the pallor and the shadows under my eyes. Looking at me was to see a younger, fatter mixture of Magnani and Moreau.

I was getting it now. I'd been in the wings. Suddenly, all the waiting had paid off, I just had to practise getting out of bed and gliding around the house in my slip and try and pull it off like Magnani had. The flesh under her arms looks fantastic!

From the films I had on video, I designed a whole wardrobe for myself – a head-to-stilettoes look.

Slept a lot, but cleaned out my room for the village seamstress.

Seamstress came up for the first time. She can do wonders with my new look. She needs two weeks and three more fittings.

✳   ✳   ✳

It was so hot last night. The crickets outside went mad, they woke me with their racket, fell asleep again very late. I dreamt the Catholic bit and it went perfectly with my look.

I'm clicking my way down an empty church, it's cool inside and my body is moist with heat.

I go straight to the confessional box and wait for the priest's voice to reach me through the grate. My make-up is perfect so, through the grate, he sees an immaculate face. I read him the list I made that morning of sins I might want to commit; and, as he reads me my Hail Mary's, I push my chest to the grille. I can feel my flesh oozing through the cold iron.

I'd been baptised as a baby in Bahia. I wasn't a practising Catholic, but I still had my calling card. Once a Catholic always a Catholic, and whatever mistakes you make, you can repent and your sins will be washed away.

The idea of good and bad excites me, and the Vatican gives you a blackboard and sponge as it takes you through its gates.

Somewhere, left over from my infancy, I have a gold cross and chain. I found them and wore them round my neck – anyway, for now.

In my dream, I was a fashion editor for Gaia, the woman from Brasil. It was lunchtime, outside, in a café in the Piazza del Popolo.

I say, `I have a new look.' There is silence. `It's all about San Gennaro, a kind of sexy Catholics out of the closet look; not stripper nuns or the equivalent, this is to be totally sensual.

It is the day of San Gennaro, there are thousands of entranced Neapolitans, who watch a group of old spinsters curse the black Madonna. They start off swearing and end up in a frenzy of sexual provocation. From the outskirts of the city, thousands of devout Catholics move in procession towards the cathedral to witness the annual miracle of San Gennaro, which is the liquefying of a phial of dried blood.

Priests intone the story of the Roman centurion who saved the city of Naples from the wrath of Mount Etna, under the shadow of the volcano. Each year, the Neapolitans succumb to mass hysteria, chanting profanities.

In the middle of this is a woman, me. (But I don't let on that it is me to anyone, of course.)

She is all dressed in black and looking good in her mourning attire. These forties suits are so flattering. In this one, my knees are bloodied, from crawling down Mount Etna. The mascara has smudged perfectly and I look as fragile, yet as sultry as you ever hope for.

I'm clutching a rosary; I lift my veil just in time to witness the miracle occurring. The crowd sighs and moans.

As the bishop holds up the test tube of liquid blood, my/her corseted breasts heave inside her immaculately tailored riding jacket, revealing a band of négligé. There is sweat on her cleavage. She's been pushed around through the frenzy and her hair has been tousled out of its pins. Her beetroot lipstick has been smudged. The frenzied women in the crowd make a circle around the bishop. They're exhausted from crawling and screaming and the heat. Clutching her rosary to her nearly bursting body, she falls to her knees — the women look like carcasses around her.

That's the shot I tell them to use: half harem, half cathedral.

CHAPTER XIX

It's time to move on.

I could stay here for ever and let the darkness swallow me up, or I could decide what I'm taking, pack, and know that from now on, if I was to go forwards, I'd have to stand on my own two stilettoes.

The obvious place to go seemed to be Rome.

I would have somewhere to stay, with my aunt
possible work – Gaia
I could visit the Vatican
I could dress up
I could slouch around the Porta Portese market
it feels near to home
it would be the perfect halfway house for someone feeling their
    way back to life

For Rome, I'd pack:

corsets
seamed stockings

slips
stilettoes
pencil skirts
clutch bags
gloves
black riding jacket
make-up
nightdresses – more forties slips
Czech wristwatch
hairpins
charm bracelet
addresses
overall and sash

I'd timed the videos so that I could keep stopping them at exactly the right point for stills. The seamstress is doing a great job.

SEPTEMBER 2ND
This morning I went down to the village for the first time since I came back. I felt a little bit like the Countess Dracula, hitting daylight after all these months.

Two seasons have slipped by.

I am seventeen.

Something reached in and stole a little piece of my life. It left a gap, now it's grown back over – like the squidgy part on a newborn baby's head.

All the leaves are falling from the trees except for the oak leaves which turn and cling. They are more resilient. They stay on the trees all winter. I am more resilient too, now.

Any day soon, Eddie's baby will be born.

In the village there is a shop with a storeroom at the back like an old emporium. For forties stuff, I didn't need any funky street markets and a sharp eye, it was all here – stacks of boxes of original stock. There were pull-me-in stockings, big French knickers and corsets for the older and fuller woman to attend weddings and funerals. Mixed in with these boxes, wrapped in dusty tissue paper, were clutch bags, big diamanté rings, brooches, clip-on veils and little powder compacts with the puff.

Despite the years of scorn I had heaped on my mother's luggage, I pulled a couple of her pre-war suitcases from under her bed to take with me. My aunt lived in Trastevere, in a flat overlooking the square. She could empty her ashtrays on the awnings of Sabatini's. I needed to remember my fox's skull, kimonos, paint brushes, school satchel, diary.

I decided to leave my manual behind. It had swelled to sixteen volumes. Everything was in it, up until Brasil. I stopped it there because that was an episode I couldn't photograph. Then I realised Eddie was right: our mother is never coming back. From now on, I'll do what other people do and instead of bringing all my life back to her, I'll take a bit of her with me, like friends do when they part.

A friend from the village drove me to the station. We stopped for an *aperitivo* at Macerata. We went back a long way, which was just as well, because he was a little bit embarrassed by the full and unabridged version of the new look, debuting that day on a station that wasn't really ready for it. By the time he'd had his arms stretched hauling my cases in and out of the underpassage and along the very long platform, he was so exhausted, he hardly noticed any more either what I was wearing or who was noticing what I was wearing. Which confirmed a lesson I had so recently learned myself: with a little bit of suffering, you can get used to a lot of things.

SEPTEMBER 10TH

I'm on my way to Rome. I'm excited about it. It's only two hours away from home, but it doesn't feel like that. Rome is another world full of:

Catholicism
candles around the bath
black veils
confession
good and evil
spaghetti alle vongole
breakfast at Sabatini's
coffee at Giorgio's
Vespa scooters
McChicken sandwiches at McDonald's in Trastevere
sit in café and look the part

Everything is changing. Last night, Cinzia appointed herself my make-up consultant. She produced bleaching and waxing products of her own and talked me through moustache control from A to Z. A girl doesn't like to think of her face as hairy, so I'd somehow managed to ignore what was going on over my upper lip during the last few months. Cinzia thinks it may have been a hot-house effect: hormones and all that darkness.

My view on the journey was criss-crossed by my veil which I had to remove when getting off the train to see the steps on to the platform.

Roma Termini station is huge. Its platforms fan out and double back so you can walk for miles. As the train pulled in, I wondered how I was going to manage with my luggage. Then I remembered my mother travelling and took strength: she never worried about our luggage, and she always had so much. Mine was only two suitcases and a hat box. Admittedly, the cases felt as though they were full of rocks.

The hat box will have to go overboard. I'm not going to get a porter. I'm going to carry my own bags.

I can see my aunt right down the other end of the platform; she can't see me. The station looks like a Turkish bazaar. To get my bags down I have to rugby tackle some other passengers. For a few minutes there is mayhem, then the scrum clears. I can do this. There are lots of things I can do now.

I step off the train and begin to walk. I am Jeanne Moreau in *Jules et Jim*, and I am Anna Magnani. I am Cat Ballou. I'm a wild woman living on my own ranch, people fear me but are intrigued by me.

I have a strong past I never talk about. I'm Modigliani's model and lover – not the one who threw herself out of the window, pregnant. I'm a peasant's daughter in the south of Italy. I'm seventeen. I'm Una. I'm me.